Penguin Books
Woolworth Mador

CW01632447

Elizabeth Troop was born in Lancashire and worked in London as a bookseller and in publishing before marrying Canadian writer and journalist Robert Troop and living in Canada for two years. She is a radio playwright and feature-writer, and her short stories have appeared in *Winter's Tales 22* and *25* and the Arts Council anthologies, as well as other magazines. Her other novels include *A Fine Country* (1969) and *Slipping Away* (1979), and her latest novel *Darling Daughters* will be published in 1980.

Elizabeth Troop

Woolworth Madonna

Penguin Books

Penguin Books Ltd,
Harmondsworth, Middlesex, England
Penguin Books, 625 Madison Avenue,
New York, New York 10022, U.S.A.
Penguin Books Australia Ltd,
Ringwood, Victoria, Australia
Penguin Books Canada Ltd, 2801 John Street,
Markham, Ontario, Canada L3R 1B4
Penguin Books (N.Z.) Ltd, 182–190 Wairau Road,
Auckland 10, New Zealand

First published by Gerald Duckworth & Co. Ltd 1976
Published in Penguin Books 1980

Copyright © Elizabeth Troop, 1976
All rights reserved

Set, printed and bound in Great Britain by
Cox & Wyman Ltd, Reading
Set in Monotype Plantin

Except in the United States of America,
this book is sold subject to the condition that
it shall not, by way of trade or otherwise, be lent,
re-sold, hired out, or otherwise circulated without
the publisher's prior consent in any form of
binding or cover other than that in which it is
published and without a similar condition
including this condition being imposed on the
subsequent purchaser

I

The dog washed his parts under the bed. Lick lick.

She could hear the milk cart whirring on the wet road. It must have rained in the night. Next door's motorbike revved up. Six a.m. regular as clockwork he was. The lousy alarm had failed to go off again. Time to wake Terry. She turned over. Let him lie a bit longer. She felt done in; another day starting, stale as her mouth.

Five minutes and she was off down the cold lino to do a pee. Pulling down her nightdress against the dawn chill. 1969 vintage, blue nylon, with a pink rosebud at the divide. Very sexy she had thought it, back in '69, but wondered even then why they had bothered with the rosebud.

In bed again she scratched her belly. Warm odours lulled her back into black unconsciousness. Mustn't drift, she thought. But did.

Christ. She had dropped off. There was the screech of the milk cart at their door, a shattering of glass. All the same, men. Glass or sperm spilled, not their responsibility. Glass got in kids' feet, sperm embedded in the womb. Not their bloody problem.

Not even light yet. No peace for the wicked. She prepared to leave the warm nest. Terry stirred, farted.

Hate sprang her out.

The kitchen greeted her with the smells of last night. Chips and vinegar Terry brought in. Disc jockeys cackled as she filled the kettle. Someone had left a wet spoon in the sugar, the granules clung like the filings on Irene's magnet. She let the cat in. He rubbed against her bare legs with his cold fur, demanding to be fed. Mangy old mog. Dirty stop-out.

She put tea bags into mugs. Pot-bellied eggs danced in the pan, leaking mucus. She put in vinegar to heal their cracks. The mucus changed into hard white balls, bulbous, attached to each egg.

She saw her reflection in a hung pan, lit by the blue gas flame. She put out her tongue at her reflection.

'Get up – you lazy lot.'

The baby howled. She was up those stairs like greased lightning.

'Mum, my egg is broken.'

'So is everybody's. Eat it.'

'But . . . I . . .'

'Eat it.'

Yellow streaked the baby's fat chapped chin. The eggs smelled of sulphur and fish as usual – whatever it was they fed them on these days – tainted.

'You kids are bog-eyed. Too much telly.'

'Don't watch as much as you do . . .'

'That's enough, Irene. Go and call your dad.'

'When I've read this. It's important.'

She plodded up herself with his orange tea, saturated with sugar. The way he liked it.

Terry rubbed his eyes, trying to focus. Looked at the clock.

'Sod you, I'm late.'

'It's your own fault, we called you. Sod you too.'

He grabbed his trousers and rushed to the bog. Downstairs he gulped a second mug of tea, trying to see the daily tit-and-bum ration in the *Sun* at the same time.

'Mind you don't choke. Tits and football keep you going.'

'Me and a million others.' He grinned at her with his charm hanging out. It didn't work, hadn't for years. He slammed the door as he left. The house shook.

She wiped their hands and faces at the sink.

'This flannel stinks. It's greasy.'

'Shut your eyes, or you'll get soap in them.'

Irene took Carole to school. It was safe to trust her, even with the motorway beginning.

'Tell Miss Arundel I'll be in later this week to see her about Carole. Don't forget, now.'

'I won't.'

'Come along, love. You have to go.'

She waved from the doorstep, Warren in her arms. Hated seeing

Carole's face, distorted in silent rage. Carole was known as 'difficult', 'backward', 'slow', and whatever it was they called them now. Maladjusted, that was it.

Her hands were red, fat red cushions. From washing. From use.

There was a moment, when the family was away, each in his or her own world, having dropped their skins, their spoor, behind while she ordered and washed and scrubbed for them; a moment when she felt such power streaming from her. It was often hate. Sometimes she felt it permeated the clothes. There was a moment when, stiffened by frost, they hung on the line like bodies, and she had killed them. Then she lifted them in, hung them over kitchen chairs to dry in the warmth. They would drip, and the cat would bat at them with his paw. She didn't want to feel that power, that love/hate, but she had got it.

Two more houses were down, the rubble rising like smoke. The big crane was swinging in. Now *there* was power. Knocking them down like a pile of children's bricks. All those years of living dissolved into thin air. You could see their wallpaper, the faded patches where mirrors and pictures had hung. Private things, all exposed, just with the swinging of a crane. The concrete of the motorway poured over like a river. As if no one had ever lived there. Like you imagine it is when they flood a Welsh valley for a reservoir.

Yet did they ever flood or concrete the rich? She didn't think so.

'Excuse me, ma'am, we are enlarging the Mall to take more traffic and so Buck House will have to go...' Not on your nellie. But the cars would glide over their past, where she had wheeled the kids, where Auntie Rose had her attack, all wasted, gone. Still, who was she to have rights over the past? It was the same for all. She remembered as a kid a day-trip to Brighton, building a castle, and the delight of seeing it destroyed by the creeping insistent sea. If they asked her now whether she would swing the crane she'd say yes. Even with the people inside. She was no longer concerned with distinctions like that.

Theirs was number thirteen. Unlucky, some would have said, and they were right, in a sense. Both Carole and Warren born here, in the back bedroom with the green paper Terry got in a job lot. Warren was named for Warren Beatty (such nice eyes). Terry was on the dole after he got the paper, and was able to put it up. She had torn at it the night Carole was born, torn it off in strips. Always meant to stick some of the spare over it, but never got around to it. Too late now. A difficult birth, the midwife had said, but didn't get Dr Jenkins round any the quicker. A busy man, she'd said, tightening her thin lips. One of the sort who thought you ought to pay for your earlier pleasure. Lots of them about. Suffer for your sins, she heard her say. You cruel cunt, she had screamed, in her bad contractions, don't you wish you'd had some, then . . . ?

Later she'd written 'I hate my life' on that wallpaper, but washed it off so that Terry wouldn't see. After all, it wasn't his fault. He would say it was a woman's thing anyway, that despair she felt. Men always thought that. Blamed it all on periods. Got your period, then? Drove her wild.

When the crane swings in they will reveal all that to the road, or what's left of it. Flakes of that wallpaper might float off and scatter, perhaps sucked into the jet stream of a jumbo, like those small birds. They do say they cause crashes. Never flown, she hadn't. Even Terry had gone to Madrid once for the football. And everybody had been to Majorca.

Next she did the socks, black from leaky Wellingtons. Irene's tights had laddered. She caught her nail in them.

Should have called her Julie, after Julie Christie. Didn't want to saddle her with a film star's name in case she wasn't pretty. But she was. So they called her Irene after Terry's mum. What a waste. Irene had a determined chin and lovely hair like Julie Christie. She didn't look in the least like Terry's mum. Thank god for it. And Warren, he wasn't at all like Warren Beatty. For a start, Warren had red hair. You couldn't win.

The pre-fabs opposite had been the first to go. Been there since the War they had. The walls were filled with the stuff you filled cushions with, she saw them, revealed. No wonder the old dears were cold.

Ma Raymond was carried off from the last of them. Didn't want to go. Her carpet slippers still in the road, filled with rubble and rainwater. Her daughter sent those slippers from Australia. She never liked them. Said you could get better at the British Home Stores. A koala bear was also sent, a mascot. She gave it to Warren, having no use for it. It frightened Warren, so Irene took it to school for nature study.

Carried off like a protester she was, Ma Raymond – well, she was one, in a sense. Not like you see on the TV, she wasn't political – but still, it took two policemen and an ambulance. She wasn't political, she just didn't want to go. Now it is flat as a field, where she was. Her roses left, bent by the bulldozer.

2

A smell of incense and curry met her at the top of the stairs. He greeted her, palms together and she sat down at the table by the window. The table was littered with dirty cups and plates. Candle grease too. She picked at it, it was spoiling his lace cloth. His brown eyes looked straight through her – they were as innocent and full of mischief as Warren's, but the irises were ringed with the white circle of the old. His beard was stained with turmeric.

He always smiled, even when the reading was bad. But it was never very bad. Otherwise people would not come. Astrologer, Palm-Reader, Shadow-Reader. How did you have your shadow read? She didn't dare ask.

'Changes here – ah, yes. Great changes.'

You could have fooled me, she thought. With a dirty great bulldozer going on outside. Changes?

'You'll have changes too,' she said, indicating the crane out of his window. He laughed. But they evicted astrologers, no doubt about it. They would knock down his pink front door, his brass plate. He wouldn't laugh then.

'Would you take some tea?' he asked. He'd never done that before.

'What kind?' She blushed. That was rude.

'Lyon's Quick Brew? O.K.?'

He went over to the sink in the corner and filled an electric kettle. She was disappointed, she expected something exotic, oriental . . . she didn't know what. It was good tea, hot and strong. Occasionally he nodded at her and smiled. He offered her a chocolate finger which she refused. She looked at his long brown hands; they had more rings than her sister-in-law's, and that was saying something.

'Where will you go, when you have to move?' She couldn't see him in a high-rise.

'It's in the lap of the gods, my dear,' he giggled. He laughed like a child, putting his hand over his mouth.

Well worth the pound. She always felt better. Cheery old sod. She wished she'd got his calm acceptance. He was a treat. Better than Librium.

The couple opposite who had boarded themselves in had been taken away while she was sipping tea. The police had not got the last of their dogs, it was still in there, behind the barricade, snapping and growling. Eight dogs, they'd had, all interbred. Part of the street, like the owners. Brother and sister, it was said. Something funny there. BEWHAIRE OF THE DOGS they painted on their barricade with aerosol paint. Then shut themselves in. There was a rumour he had a shotgun. Mrs Dawes, who knew all that went on, said they were to be parted, one to a male and the other to a female old folks' home. Then Mrs Dawes said however *she* thought they was both male. Now how could that be?

She brought the geranium cuttings in, the last of the sun had warmed them. She sniffed her fingers, they smelled of bitter lemon. The leaves were like velvet rubbed the wrong way, strange to the touch.

Warren was still asleep. She woke him, feeling to see if he was soaked. He was. She shouldn't have left him while she went to the Yogi – one day something would happen to punish her. Warren had torn a bit more off the green wallpaper; his mother's son. His face, red and sore from crying, told her he had been frustrated by her absence.

She hugged him, shoved him into his push chair. A bit of chocolate would shut him up, his mouth was puckering into crying position. Most kids seemed to feel anguish when they were woken. Who didn't?

She would run with the push chair, down the derelict road. Make him laugh.

WHEEEE!

Look at your mum, she cried. The all-round entertainer.

3

The school was red-brick, Victorian. Iron railings. An asphalt yard. The same as when she was there, MIXED INFANTS and JUNIORS over two entrances. A usual selection of mums congregated outside the gates; carpet slippers and rollers with scarves tied over them, fake furs and boots, even a smattering of tweed coats and headscarves from the new house-buying fraternity who were said to be 'improving' the area. No one spoke to them – it wasn't worth it. They sent their kids to MIXED INFANTS but removed them before JUNIORS, getting scared about accents and such. They farmed out their offspring, to Putney and Richmond, a bit of a drive away.

There was nothing to do, waiting, except study the new crop of rude words. DAVE IS A WANKER seemed to be the only addition. She watched a young mum in jeans try out a hop-and-a-jump on the chalked pavement, but the poor girl saw her watching and stopped. Warren splashed about in a puddle; his yellowing nappy dragged out of his plastic pants.

It seemed she had stood here for years, a statue, rain and shine.

Had she guessed this was the way it would turn out?

No.

Since Carole she didn't see why she owed it to the world to approve of it. Funny, though, no one had noticed the change in her attitude.

Warren staggered over to the coal shute. Boudicca Sykes had once pushed Carole down there. What a name, Boudicca. Strong as a horse, like her mother – her mother resembled one. Did market research, could be found standing on the High Street with a large board and sheaf of notes asking questions about radio programmes, soap powders and sex. Once Boudicca Sykes' mother had asked her (not for research) what she thought a woman's role was, and she had answered, stuck here like a lemon, day after day. Boudicca's mum had whinnied. She supposed they were building a pattern. A pattern, no matter how badly formed. Funny. No one had bothered to do it for her and Terry. They fell between generations. Now all the books were on how to be a good parent; when their parents was young, it had been all the other way. No one was an expert parent; stuck in the pubs they were, and chips for the family dinner all week. Now it was like the TV advertisements . . . if you didn't have the whitest knickers, you was a failure.

You pretended it was otherwise, but unless you won the Pools what chance had you of getting out of it? Like a bloody squirrel's cage – round and round.

Irene danced over the asphalt, a piece of paper in her hand. Grey, soft paper, with bright colours over it and drawing-pin marks in each corner.

'You had it pinned up? Let's see . . .'

Irene smelled of chalk and urine, the smell of primary school. The rain spattered down, spotting the picture, making the colours run.

'Got a gold star for it – see . . .' she boasted.

'Such a clever – such clever girls I have.' For Carole was in earshot. It didn't do to praise Irene in front of her – it was difficult enough for her. Carole gave her a weak smile. Some wouldn't have rated it a smile, but it was as good as she ever gave. Should she be more pleased over that than the picture? Christ.

Irene sighed, handing over the painting to be put in the shopping bag. She was used to keeping her talents dark.

'Miss Arundel said see her today, Mum.'

'Oh, why? Do I have to?'

She grabbed Warren. Wheeled him in, against the tide of children. Miss Arundel was at her desk. One of those fresh, eager faces that thought they knew what to do about everything on this earth – but a lot less fresh than it had been two years ago. Miss Arundel smiled her bad news.

'She can't keep up with the others. You were right. It was worth a try, though, don't you agree?'

'It isn't your fault dear. She's always been like that.'

Very kind, denying her own child to comfort the teacher. Still, she looked tired.

'We are going to discuss what should be done. Special schools are really the best thing for . . .'

'Children like Carole.'

'Could you and your husband come and discuss it, if I make an appointment with the headmaster?'

Carole was banging the desk with a ruler. Relentlessly. Neither of them attempted to stop her.

And now Miss Arundel was flying past on her white-painted bicycle, all flying scarves and skirts. She waved, nearly causing a major pile-up. The rain was bucketing down. Families sheltered in doorways. She liked rain, it made her feel sexy, warm inside her gut. Warren sucked his thumb, frowned, threatening as the sky. Irene moaned about homework. Carole's face was closed-off. Who knew what she thought? The funny thing was, she felt this mounting sense of excitement. *She had a letter in her pocket. She would never dare post it.* It could go off like a bomb if she wanted it to. She luxuriated in the feeling. The red buses, shimmering on the wet road pleased her, the brightness of the odd plastic mac as people hurried past. It was the feeling she had at school in art lessons, when the ordinary objects around seemed filled with radiance – just because you saw them, for a split second, in a different light. She didn't have that feeling much any more.

When she lifted the kids out of the kitchen sink, in the evening, dripping and slippery from the soap, they seemed to her beautiful, like roses. Over the stink of old fat, the steamy emulsioned walls, the dirty dishes, they emerged, blooming.

She felt the same now. People in the rain. Beauty. Whatever it was, and she didn't know what it was, was what counted.

'Sod it, Mum. We're getting wet.'

'Don't say "sod it", Irene.'

'You do.'

She took hold of Carole's icy little hand, and ran.

Her own body she avoided if she could. Sallow and slack-bellied it was. She had a quick up-and-down wash as quickly as possible at the kitchen sink. Generations of her lot had done without bathrooms. Now she had one, it was too damp to use. What a laugh.

She did bathe there when they first moved in. Would wait for Terry after, sitting up in the big brass bed her gran had left her. When the kids were on the way he would rub her belly with olive oil, to stop stretch marks appearing. She could still feel the sensation; his hand, the warm oil cupped in the palm, and him slapping it on to her swelled flesh. The baby would ripple slowly, like someone moving underwater. Is my hand too cold? he would ask, and she would laugh, because it tickled. Now? Now the veins stood out on her legs and her belly muscles had gone. Who cared? If he put his hand on her now she didn't want to know.

As for him, thickening, getting a corporation, hanging out of his pyjamas. Combed his hair forward, a small vanity. Use to be proud of his body. Exercised, preened. Couldn't say she had helped in that direction. It didn't exactly inspire his self-confidence to have her nit-picking comments, her sexual refusals.

He'll end up a dour old man, she thought. Trek down to the pub at opening time, lunchtime and night, like all the grey ones; never getting drunk enough.

Even winning the Pools wouldn't help them now.

The sad thing: sometimes his face lit up like a little boy's, when he turned to her in the night, hopefully. Or when Chelsea won.

The rain had stopped. They straggled along, the four of them, home.

4

Warren, egg-smeared, kissed the telly lady goodnight. Irene rushed at him, dragging him away, saying he would be electrocuted. He screamed; the noise went through her head like the road drill outside. She slapped Irene. Her hand left a red imprint on the child's astonished face.

She lit a fag, sat on the step. Breathed slowly in and out, to control her temper. Good for the nerves, they taught her that at the yoga class. In the town hall, all those bulging matrons in tights and sagging jumpers, heaving and sweating, it had put her right off. Nothing to do with the mysterious East, that lot.

She had forgotten the letter in her raincoat pocket.

The unfinished parts of the motorway flashed out warning lights in the distance. Red lanterns gave it a carnival atmosphere. Would the fumes from the new road, and the noise, reach up to those high rise blocks, she wondered? She could smell the fumes now, and it wasn't even half-ready. They moved slowly, like an approaching army. Sometimes they worked at night, the bang and clatter under the floodlights made it have an importance it didn't show in the day. Powerful; how she imagined the modern world ought to be, how she thought it was in America. Would it be different, America? Not for her kind. She'd be as stuck there as here, wouldn't she? Roads, kids, squalor. It was all the same. Why think this way – defeated? She should get a bottle of light ale. The little magic pills were running out. She was tired of feeling damped-down anyway. Green and yellow perils. God bless the National Health Service and all who float on her.

Did she even care where they moved to next? She had to. Who else was there? Oh, they kidded you on the television documentaries, but let's face it, you were in a long, a globe-long queue. Most people looked after number one and who could blame them? People who love people are the sickest people in the world. She'd sing it that way.

Did it seem to her that she'd had a revelation? Damn right it didn't.

The kids had fiddled with the faulty TV knob and the pictures on the two channels they watched moved round as if on a crazy spool so that they were dizzy and had to switch off. Later on, Terry at the pub, she had watched the other channel, the one they never had on. It was a talk, and an orchestra playing modern music, not jazz, not classical either. She had seen him for the first time, the man with the foreign name, MROZEK. Of course she'd seen conductors before, André Previn's Music Night and all that. But this was different.

It was complicated, and the images and musical symbols and the French poem he was explaining danced madly in front of her eyes. If she concentrated she suddenly remembered a bit of French she had learned in her two years at the Grammar. She didn't feel an idiot any more. And the eyes held her – the penetrating eyes of Mrozek.

Here's a good programme, Terry, she had called as he arrived home. Told him his dinner was hot in the oven. He looked in, asked if the TV was fixed yet – there was some wrestling on later. She said the man hadn't been to repair it; heard the scraping of the dinner into the bin, the slam of the back door. Looked up again into the eyes of Mrozek. They continued their rapt flirtation; he explaining, she absorbing.

That had started it. Excitement, a heightened response to life. She, going stupid over a fellow on the television. She heard a bit of the piece he had been talking about when she listened to Irene's transistor while she was making the beds.

Then the magnetic photographed eyes of Mrozek startled her over the supermarket bargain record display. It was as if he had followed her. She bought the record, putting back the round steaks and picking up mince. Their record player was bust – she put the record at the back of her wardrobe. It was her secret. There was a biography of Mrozek on the back, he was Polish, had studied in Vienna, had been in America, was coming to live in London. *Here.* This cheered her – she couldn't think why.

She tried to write to him, like some besotted groupie.

'Dear Mr Mrozek . . . I . . .'

She – what?

Knew nothing about music. Liked his eyes?

'Dear Mr Mrozek . . . You . . .'

He what? Excited her, interested her – made her life . . . what?

She had nothing to offer.

'Dear Sir, I enjoyed your programme on –' What were they . . . Ravel songs?

She was stupid. Terry was right.

'Dear Mrozek . . . I wouldn't mind fucking you.' That was more like the truth.

What a moron. Not ready for culture.

She had the letter in her pocket – she would never dare send it.

Mrozek. She began to dream about Mrozek.

5

Some days she spent hours looking at recent sleeves and magazines, hoping to catch the magic name of Mrozek. A stupid obsession.

She did sketches of him – tore them up.

But didn't Terry look at the furry cunts in *Playboy* with the same eye? She supposed that to him it was the same. A fantasy ... and so was a balding East European conductor. Old enough to know better, aware of her state, she persisted. Her fantasy didn't keep her going, it accentuated the misery, kept her aware of her discontent. Her fantasy was difficult, it made her feel worthless, insignificant. Sometimes she thought it would drive her round the bend, but she was too responsible to let it. Her type didn't go mad. She knew what reality was.

Reality was the time she met Terry. Each day seemed to have a purpose, because at the end she saw him. Had to touch him, marvel in the fact of his existence. The old trap, the biological urge shared by each couple in the back row of the cinema. The fumblings and touchings, the fantasy fucking. Frustrated by the flash of the manager's torch, revealing flushed faces, empty cartons, dog-ends, discarded wrappers. Afterwards, a milk bar, juke box blaring – puddles of tea on formica tops, the waitress with a stenchy rag. Romantic. The walk along the High Street, looking at furniture in bright windows. Available on Easy Terms. Planning the luxury of a double bed, kissing in doorways. Not wanting to relinquish the hold on the other. Had that been real? She thought so.

And in the early days of marriage, the firelight, the breathing-in of the other, the peace. The act of sex no longer furtive, but allowed to flower. Kept in check by natural modesty and shyness which suddenly appeared. The secrecy too; they were in rented rooms, and the grunting and moaning they heard through the thin walls told them that passion was often a ludicrous thing when objective. On the other side of the wall it sounded obscene.

Her stomach used to lurch when she saw him. She had left the

Grammar and taken a job at Woolworth's, on the record counter. Irene was on the way. Irene turned inside her like a wave in the sea. She felt anguished when she turned away from him the first time, through pregnancy, and hated his reaction. She still had the memory of the feeling when he came and put his hand on the back of her neck. After a day on the building site he was tanned, dusty, tired.

She would strip the clothes off him, trace with her finger where the tan ended and the pale white flesh began. His body burned her up more than the sun that summer. They rested like two birds on the bed, his hand on her crotch, hers on his prick.

But when the baby came the bed was always cold and damp from Irene's pee and the overflow of milk from her abundant breasts. Terry moved over, hunched up on his own remote side of the bed. He had never returned, not in the same way.

She remembered him suckling her full breast – like condensed milk he said it was. He had spread it on bread when he was a boy. She had laughed then, feeling like mother earth; one on each tit. That stage didn't last long.

Hostile since then, on the whole. Though it was possible to pretend a bit when necessary. Now even that had gone. Warren's birth had pleased him. A boy at last – after those clefted creatures.

Carole had got the worst of it – born at a bad time, and marred. Her difficulty was the last straw – men don't like difficulties. He wouldn't hurt her for the world. He just didn't know he was rejecting her. She hugged Carole time and time again, telling her she was pretty. She was, too.

They had fucked like robots after Carole's birth. No love. He seemed to be trying to prove something. She didn't conceive, though. Then, after two years of this torture, Warren.

He wasn't too clever about favouring Warren. There wasn't much Irene didn't take in. She would make it – whatever that meant.

Terry would think her off her rocker if she talked of Irene making it. Lazy sod. She was the one who got things going. She got up the protest to save the street, but it was too late. They all signed, all the old dears, but she guessed they weren't important – not to stand in the way of a road. Still, there was a picture in the local paper; they never heard nothing after that. Sitting in front of the television isn't going to get you anywhere, she would shout at Terry, but he just gave her two fingers up in the air.

Why had Terry married her? He was always in awe of the fact she'd been to the Grammar. Anyway, she'd left soon enough. But he felt inferior, and wouldn't admit it. Always eyed the local tarts in the pub. That ex-TV Topper, all platinum highpiled hair like whipped cream, admired by all the blokes because of her legs and her dirty line of talk. Like dogs after a bitch they were. Do a bit more to yourself, can't you? he asked. And look like a bloody meringue, she said.

She had brown hair and thick legs (they didn't used to be) and she looked as if she belonged in a Russian film starring her and a tractor. (Perhaps it might appeal to Mrozek, her style? No, men were the same the world over.)

She liked the autumn. You could pull the curtains early, settle in and dream. Shut out the world. Is that what she wanted? It had the feel of a battlefield around here, she thought – but where's the bloody war? Perhaps they were the last survivors. Felt as derelict as the partly demolished houses herself. Was she marked-out for it – this *nothing*? Perhaps it could have been forecast from the sepia snaps, taken with a box Brownie – a big-mouthed eager kid, squinting into the sun? Was she destined to do bugger-all with her life?

She shivered, turned on all the lights. She wondered if she could listen to that concert from Salzburg. Terry might go to the pub, then she could listen to the radio downstairs. They did say it was lovely and warm in the high-rises, but expensive. Under-floor heating. No one liked to admit they couldn't afford the bills. All the women worked. It would be a new life. Modern. They did say the lifts were filled with human shit, but you couldn't believe all you heard. Teenagers vandalized; but Irene would soon be a teenager, and she wasn't like that.

The modulated tones of the announcer alternated with scenes of violence and floated up the stairs. Warren was mounting them to find her.

'Maa . . .' Sounded like a goat.

'Watch it, pet. Careful.'

She swept him up into her arms.

'Ever heard of Bruckner, you little bugger? Or Mrozek? There – let's wipe your nose. You don't care, do you? Let's go down and get the supper for your dad . . .'

6

As it was half-term and she didn't know what to do with the kids she decided to be revolutionary and take them to the South Bank for a picnic. It would be better to leave Carole behind – she was so difficult in public, sometimes having a tantrum on the train or tube. The church hall nursery school would take her – they weren't aware she had started primary school and she was happy with the younger ones, piddling around with finger paints and plasticine. She never even looked up when they left her.

It wasn't much of a day. The power station loomed like a dirty cardboard castle. They got the train to Waterloo. Warren on her knee, staring with his insulting implacable gaze, never responded to lively conversations with adults, much as they tried. He was thinking 'fuck you'.

Irene jiggled up and down, making knowing remarks about the passing scene to attract attention. When no one appeared to be listening she drew moodily on the dirty window, faces, words . . .

At the station they bought chocolate from a slot machine, not forgetting some to take back to Carole. Carole's face imposed itself wherever she went – sometimes it was worse than having her there. You get used to guilt. She was becoming an expert at ignoring it. Couldn't have handled three of them. The one to have left was Warren; she shrugged, to get rid of the thought. Irene told her to stop twitching.

She loved the sudden rush of people at stations. All different, never to be seen again in the same arrangement. Like that kaleidoscope they got Carole for her birthday. (Carole again.) A Nigerian in gold headdress and brown and black robe. Bowler-hatted blokes, late for the office, running to the ridiculous militant march coming out of the loudspeakers. Derelicts and drifters, prone on benches, or sorting out the day's rubbish from the litter bins. A thin old lady fed nuts to the pigeons.

'She was here when I came with the school,' Irene said. 'Does she live here?'

'She might well. Isn't it exciting?' she asked.

'*What?*' said Irene.

'All this.'

'They're only *people*,' said Miss Sophisticate.

Kids could be very arrogant, they never seemed to share your enthusiasm.

'Isn't it nice to be going somewhere for once?'

Irene scowled.

They followed the arrows indicating the Festival Hall and Hayward Gallery. She had read there was an old man mugged along there the other day, stabbed by a junkie. It stank of urine, that passage, and she rushed through, pushing Warren, urging Irene to hurry. *There*, smiling down at her from a poster, Mrozek. *His hand was raised to the invisible orchestra*. It was like a greeting. She beamed.

'What are you grinning at, mum?'

'That's my business.'

'Meanie . . . meanie . . . meanie . . .'

Irene's voice echoed through the arcade.

Along by the concert hall they went; Irene making straight for the river, leaning over to watch the barges pass. The Thames was flowing fast, carrying a mass of effluvia along as if on a conveyor belt; the eye could hardly follow it. Driftwood, plastic bottles, crates, old cans, the large branch of a tree, the dead orange leaves of autumn still on it. They played a game, picking out something and watching to see how quickly it went.

'That bit of blue plastic . . . no, it's too small. That petrol can.'

'There it goes . . . I can't see it any longer.'

'And there's a balloon. Look mum, a little balloon.'

'I can't see a balloon.'

'You need glasses. There it goes. Good-bye, balloon.'

It was a condom.

*

'Hungry?'

She put out the sandwiches. Peeled an orange for Warren and gave it to him, piece by piece.

People were eating lunch in the Festival Hall cafeteria, looking out at them from the big glass windows. Irene jumped up and down and gibbered, scratching her armpits.

'Irene – stop it. Sit down.'

'They look at me as if I'm a monkey. So I am one.'

'I won't tell you again.'

Warren ran his car down the slope. She wondered if Carole was all right. At the Hayward Gallery they could see some of the sculpture on the sculpture court if they looked up. Irene said they were like coloured drainpipes.

The wind howled around those concrete buildings. Tears ran down their faces, from the cold. It was eerie, as if King Kong might swing around one of the pillars to scare them. They played horror films; she rushed after Irene, pushing the squealing Warren in front of her. Then she hid with him, and pounced. But it wasn't Irene she collided with, but a young man. She grabbed him to stop herself falling. He asked anxiously if she was hurt. Apart from cracking her shin on the push chair, she was fine. Warren was yelling blue murder.

The stranger was one of those denim-suited types, with a straggly fair moustache. Irene peered at him from behind a pillar.

'Not hurt, I hope?'

'No.'

Irene smiled at him with her best smile.

'And mother?'

She tried not to wince. Her shin was beginning to bleed.

'I'm fine. Really.'

'You must come and have a coffee, just in here. Please.'

'With this lot? No thank you.'

He persuaded her to sit down inside, where the telephones were. Irene went and started picking out notices of concerts.

'Put that lot back now.'

'Oh, she can take some. You can draw on the backs, can't you?'

'Mm.'

The young man bit his nails. She was aware of him glancing at her. What did they look like, the three of them? She was so ashamed.

She stood up.

'We really have to go.'

'I'll drive you. Look, my car is just out there.'

'Oh, *please* mum . . . say yes.'

'It's no trouble. Just tell me where you live.'

'Well, just to the station, then. Waterloo. If you really don't mind.' Just before she left she cast a glance back at the poster. The dark eyes of Mrozek were following her, just like they did on that picture, the Laughing Cavalier.

Irene, Warren and she bundled into the back, the push chair perched beside him on the front seat. He switched on the cassette recorder and music flooded the car.

'What's that?' she asked.

'Mrozek's Figaro.'

Natural as anything. *Mrozek*. Before they had time to settle in, they were there.

'Thanks,' she said shyly.

'It could have been the whole way.'

'Thanks anyway . . .'

He waved as he drove off. Irene sighed.

'If I had a car, I'd play pop, not that boring music. Wasn't he nice?'

'He was alright.'

You shouldn't ever try and come out – change your life from the humdrum, it only made you worse. The excitement she had felt on seeing the poster was dispersed. The young man had whipped her away from Mrozek's presence. She'd have to go back, without them. Her leg ached. Warren began to howl, and she clouted him. Irene came rushing over and told her off. Why did it all look so meaningless now, this afternoon? She was late for Carole, too. Carole – she hadn't thought about her for hours.

Irene drew faces on the window again. Someone had scrawled CHELSEA RULES O.K. on the Life Assurance advertisement.

The ad featured a happy family sheltering under a large umbrella with the insurance company name written on it.

She hoped no one would get in, but fate, knowing how she felt, sent her nosey Mrs Dawes at Clapham Junction. She puffed up to their compartment, having seen Irene at the window.

'Hello my love, having a day out?'

The CIA and the KGB combined, that was Mrs Dawes.

'You are late today, Mrs Dawes . . .' Mrs D was a cleaner at one of the big office blocks near Waterloo.

'You're looking down in the mouth, ducks. Did you know your leg was bleeding?'

'Caught it on the push chair.'

'We went for a ride in a posh car,' carolled Irene.

'Did you my love?'

Luckily Mrs Dawes never took in what children said; her generation didn't. Because if she had, Terry would have heard about the young man and there would be hell to pay.

'Terry all right, is he? In work? Your Carole isn't playing up, is she?' Probing. The Dawes technique. She should have a TV interview spot.

'Just leave me alone. I'll be alright.'

Tears rolled down.

'Sorry, I'm sure.'

Her reflection bounced back at her from the train window. Puffy, lined. If the Mrozek poster sprang to life this is what he would see. She was tied to this; her particular life. It had never hit her before. It had happened without her willing it. But if she wanted to fight it, that would be worse, because she was defeated before she started. All there was, was here, now. If she chucked herself into that brown river over there all that would happen would be a line or two in the local rag.

Wandsworth Mother of Three Found in Thames – the body of a woman aged between twenty-five and forty was washed up on the foreshore today. She was wearing a gold wedding ring. There were no identifying marks. Her clothes consisted of an anorak, a black and brown Harris tweed skirt, red polo necked sweater, tights, black shoes. The police say there is no evidence of foul play.

Irene had traces of chocolate around her mouth. Mrs Dawes had slipped her a Mars bar. She hoped Irene wasn't planning one of her reports to Terry, the fact that they'd had a lift (Terry was jealous, always had been), or that she had hit Warren. Irene could be very officious.

Mrs Dawes collected her package.

'Sorry if I was rude. Must be getting the 'flu or something.'

'Forget it, my love. I know how it is, moving and that. You and your Terry should come and look at our Jayne's flat. Real nice. Of course the kids scare her, trying to undo the window latches, but you might not get such a high one. She's got over her dizzy feeling with the pills. You come and see . . .'

She promised. Made Irene walk Mrs Dawes home to carry the parcels. Irene wasn't keen.

She got a cool reception at the church hall. Carole was sitting with her coat on. Mrs Gale was opposite Carole, reading *Woman's Journal.*

'I must say this is very annoying,' Miranda Gale began.

'I had to take Warren to the hospital. And she won't be coming again. She goes to the primary now.'

'Well, really. She shouldn't be here at all. They took her, then?' Mrs Gale collected her handbag and coat. 'Do you remember the little chat we had . . .'

'I remember.' Miranda Gale had suggested Carole should have some sort of tests.

'Here.' She took a crumpled pound note out of her pocket. 'For your trouble . . .'

Miranda Gale flushed.

'You know I can't take that. I . . . well, I have my own children to see to. You're very late.'

'Then take it and buy your kids an ice cream. Hospitals keep you waiting hours . . . It isn't my fault.'

Watched her squirm. Mrs Gale, ex-RADA, now doing up her terraced house. She stuck the pound under a pot of anemones.

'I'll see it gets used for some new finger paints,' she announced.

'Please yourself. Come on, Carole.'

'Good luck at the primary, Carole,' said Miranda Gale. She wasn't really put out about the pound. The Gales of the world never were.

She was angry at herself. She knew what they all thought of Carole, and throwing away a pound didn't do any good. She'd heard them chattering one day. At first she thought they said Carole was artistic, and was pleased. Then she realized with horror that the word was *au*tistic. Well, she'd seen the programme too. It wasn't true. Carole wouldn't speak, but that was because of her lip – not that it wasn't cured, it was, but it had held her back. She was a bit shy. Withdrawn? No, shy. And she did have tantrums. But so did a lot of kids. She was just – shy.

'Here's some raisins from the machine, love,' she said. Carole grabbed them. She wasn't backward.

Apart from the blood drying on her shin, and the sweet pain of a beginning bruise, she was going to lose all trace of the morning, of Mrozek.

She opened her mouth to protest, to scream; but saw Warren and Irene watching her. She closed it again, like a goldfish.

7

She was hanging on to Terry, riding his storm, wondering why it left her so unaffected. It was something to do with optimism, and with trust; there had been a time she hoped, and trusted in him.

'Here, I've lost you – what's going on?'

'Just stay there,' she urged. 'Move around, but be quiet. You'll wake Warren. I just don't feel like it much, these days.'

There was a time when she used to grip him with her thighs like one of those posh girls on a pony, urging him. Now her indifference was hard to hide.

He started to move inside her again. She mechanically with him, up and down, in and out, round and round. Never make love with dry loins – a student she had gone with once told her that. Not that she ever had, then. Was it self-disgust that made her feel dead? The dead quality was taking her over. Like a shaft of steel, right through her, needle-thin, but there all right. Her flesh surrounded it, making her seem normal. No one knew. Wrong. Terry knew.

Perhaps she could conjure up old lusts, old feelings. Or think of –, no, that was obscene. He shuddered, had his final thrust inside her, sprang out, ejaculated. Hit or miss. She turned her head away. He turned his head away.

'God, what did you want to do that for?' Sorry for him now, comforting. The usual role.

'I'm sorry,' he said, not sounding it.

'I don't mind, but you usually say. Or wait for me.'

'You didn't seem to care, either way. Or even be there. So I pleased myself.'

It was true. Another time over, she'd been thinking. Hadn't even bothered to pretend, at his coming climax; just let him get on with it. But she never thought of him, or imagined his face, Mrozek. That would have betrayed Terry.

He was looking for cigarettes in her drawer. He might find the picture, or the scrawled letters she'd never sent.

'Terry – '

'What?'

'I've got some here, in my bag.'

'What's up with you these days, you're dreaming half the time. Chuck them over.'

'Aren't you coming back to talk?'

'What's there to talk about . . .'

'I'm just unsettled. The move.'

'Everybody else has had to do it – what's so special about you?'

'That's it, isn't it. If you thought we was a bit special we'd . . .'

'We'd what? Grow up.'

'You make me feel like a load of rubbish. You leave me high and dry.'

'It takes two, didn't anyone ever tell you?'

Warren breathed noisily through his mouth. They were awake, back to indifferent back. It was three a.m.

'You know we have to go to the school tomorrow, about Carole. You haven't forgotten?'

'Don't get on to me now.'

'Just don't forget it, that's all. She's not getting on as she should.'

'She's shy.'

'She's not bloody shy. It's more than that.'

'You think she's simple. You'll be saying she gets it from me next.'

'They don't call it simple these days . . .'

'Well, I'm not so up on these things as you. Not much education you know. Retarded then.'

'Not retarded. Maladjusted.'

'I'll give them maladjusted when I see them.'

'You? That'll be the day. You won't open your trap. Yes sir, no sir, three bags full, sir.'

She could see she had got to him. The little vein in his forehead was twitching.

'Stands to reason they know more than we do. They're professionals.'

She gave him some mock-applause.

'That's my boy. I said you wouldn't open your trap.'

'Perhaps I got more respect than you . . .'

'Oh, you're full of it. Know what Irene says? "What do they know – they're not so clever . . ." And that's your own daughter. Got more balls than you have.'

'I don't know what you want me to do.' He was sweating. 'How do I know what's wrong with her?'

'All I want is to discuss it.'

'I'd like to discuss what went on in here tonight. In this bloody bed.'

'What always goes on, a lot of nothing.'

She'd hurt him this time.

'What the hell are you playing at, anyway? Got a new bloke have you? Don't think I haven't noticed.'

'Hundreds. They queue up all day outside. While the kids are at school. Warren watches from his cot.'

He ignored that.

'Have you done?' he finally said. 'Because I'd like to get some sleep.'

'And Terry – ' she said . . .

'What?'

'I'm sorry. I do *try* . . .'

It was the wrong thing to say. He punched her in the face. She didn't cry out because of Warren.

'Don't try then. Or try harder.'

He was over her, pressing her down. She widened her legs, there was no use opposing him, she would only get hurt. A bit of blood from her wounded mouth smeared his shoulder. They clung like wrestlers on the television, grunting and heaving. Well, she thought, if I can't be human, I'll have to be a shit. Think of Mrozek? She couldn't, in the circumstances, conjure up Mrozek's face.

'Have I hurt you?' Terry asked. It was over. Gentle now. Oh yes, kind now. The trouble was, he would think something had been repaired. Had to show his authority. The way he'd been brought up. 'The wife.' He probably did say it, down at the pub. They all did, still. Thought it had died out, like the music hall. No.

'Terry – '

She had to get him while he was satisfied.

'We have to do something.'

'We just done it.' He laughed. She didn't. 'About what, love?'

'Our lives.'

'Must we talk about it now?' His voice was full of pain.

'When else do I get your attention?'

He moved his arm from under her.

'I'm coming to the school tomorrow. I promise.' He began to stroke her breasts again. The nipples sprang up automatically, she could have killed them.

'I'm tired, Terry. Enough is enough.'

'I love coming into you. It's so warm and safe. The best place in the world.'

'You make me sound like an old armchair.'

'You should be grateful. Look.'

'I've seen it before. One of nature's little miracles.'

But he had her, and he knew it. She watched him stir and grow large and put her hand on him.

'Let me just do it this way . . .'

'No. He wants *her*.'

And had her. Three times a night. Ridiculous she told herself.

So, had he exorcized Mrozek?

Had she?

*

It was no good, she wouldn't sleep now. She picked up Warren, who was whimpering. She had to be careful, getting out from under the huge arm, sliding out of bed. Warren was wet through. She made her way downstairs.

She loved the middle of the night. The house was crumpled and worn, it had possibilities. She sat with Warren on her lap, read the evening paper. Pedro shuffled down, thinking it was morning. He banged his dish. She ignored him, and he settled at her feet, turning in circles as he always did. The light was filtering in through the curtains. She made a cup of tea and sat with the wet bulk of her child on her lap, sipping the sugary brew.

Funny she'd had a ride in a car with a strange bloke. She didn't fancy him, not at all.

She lost herself in a fantasy of meeting Mrozek, not elaborating, just feeling the pressure of a hand on her shoulder, his dark eyes penetrating hers. How stupid could you get? She reached over for a clean nappy for Warren, laid him on the table. His legs unfolded, his small sex curled and delicate, like they did them on statues. She tried to remember the concert she'd heard on the radio yesterday. Couldn't. She had the music programme on all day now. You learned a lot.

Why did their lot prefer the trash? She had been forced to leave the Grammar School but there wasn't any of the Mrozek thing there. She would have become a teacher if she'd gone on. Perhaps she could still do that. What, without O levels? She felt she could do it, in the middle of the night, on her own. But it was different in the morning.

Suppose her kids did no better? Oh, Irene would. Terry was happy, the kids and her. Made him feel a man. When she let him. But when he got old – what will he have had? When working men go, they go quick. Their hardness changing into false-toothed cheeriness. Or beeriness. Beer bellies. She'd seen it. Opening time, closing time. Gardening, if they had gardens. None of them would have, in the future.

Terry's dad had aged well. An old dear. A gentle man. Often surprised her; he was very courteous with women. Knew bits of poetry. Quoted them at her. World War I poems . . . 'Ever again to breathe pure happiness, the happiness our mother gave us boys? To smile at nothings, needing no caress.' Oh, a sweet old man.

The only poetry Terry knew was Eskimo Nell.

She'd have to go back up, she'd be a wreck in the morning. Warren was peaceful, she laid him in the cot. There, my lamb, clean and fresh. She looked in on the girls – Irene was sleeping purposefully, as she did everything. Carole had restless dreams, her voice, unheard in the day, often soared with strange cries at night. In the day she mimed her wants, at night she was released. Sprawled out, she frowned. It was a strain for her, the constant near-communication.

Warren's bright eyes followed her as she went back into their bedroom. She held her breath, if he wanted to start playing up he would wake the lot of them. The eyes slowly shut. His thumb went in like a cork in a bottle. She removed it, gently. He replaced it.

Her place was still warm. So we go on, day after day, she thought.

She didn't want them Mozarts . . . it was just . . .

Yawned.

Hell, why be so timid. She wanted them Mozarts!

(*If they wanted to be, that is . . .*)

8

Terry kept his promise, they were at the school next evening. She had to laugh, seeing him sitting at one of those little tables on a tiny chair gazing up at Miss Arundel. She had a terrible cold, poor girl, her small nose was red and swollen.

'So sorry – if you could find Carole's classroom, yes, well . . . I'll just see if I can find Mr Jackson, you go on in . . .'

They did as they were told.

'You didn't tell me she was pretty. I'd have been along before.'

'Now, don't forget. Be dominant. We're here to fight for Carole.'

She walked round, looking at the bright paintings on the walls. Kids do great paintings, she thought, all wild and free. Before they become rigid and get timid about what they want to express. Seeing them gave her a pang. She had been good at art. Would like to have discussed with

Miss Arundel how you got to be a primary teacher, but tonight was Carole's. When Miss Arundel came in she asked if there was anything of Carole's they could see.

'Well, no. Carole hasn't wanted to paint.'

'She used to love to finger-paint at the nursery group.'

'Well, we can't get her to do it here. Measuring and weighing, she likes that.'

'Is that all she does?' asked Terry.

'She's rather a law unto herself – as you probably know ...' Miss Arundel said. 'Of course, it might be me. I'm not very experienced, after all.'

'Oh, I'm sure you know what you are doing,' said Terry quickly. She looked daggers at him. Terry drummed his fingers on the little table.

'Alright to smoke, is it?'

'Terry. Not here ...'

Miss Arundel smiled.

'Oh, go ahead. He doesn't approve, but he'll just think it is me. I have to light up sometimes or I'd go crazy.'

'I won't if it'll get you in trouble. Wouldn't like to see you get the cane.'

Delighted by that, Miss A. Sexy under the long skirts.

'Don't you think we should talk about Carole? That's what we're here for.'

They both looked at her. Her voice had been very sarcastic, among the pleasantries, the paint daubs, the model Wombles.

'Would you like to see some of Carole's workbooks?' Miss Arundel moved over to the white cupboard with daisies painted on it. 'Here ...'

She reached out and intercepted the notebook.

They scanned it together. Most of the pages were blank, but on some of them a thin scrawl, as if a snail had trailed across.

'Perhaps we could see some other child's book – just to compare,' said Terry. Miss Arundel fished one out at random. The exercise book was just like Carole's except that the beginning letters and the beginning drawings had an ordered mind behind them.

'There isn't much difference. Is there, Terry?'

'No,' he lied. They all knew.

'It is just a question of manual dexterity,' said Miss Arundel. 'And a little bit lacking in concentration. Now whether she can, and isn't doing it, or whether she really can't ... at this stage it is impossible to tell. It's too early. She may resent me. Personal relationships matter in the first year. Does she speak much at home?'

'Yes,' said Terry.

'*No.*'

Weighed and found wanting, she thought, touching the little scales and measures Carole liked. She had never felt such searing pain.

The headmaster rushed down the passage, he was anxious to help, and anxious to get home – he worked a twelve- to fourteen-hour day.

'Now, it's about Irene –'

'Carole,' corrected Miss Arundel, dabbing at her nose.

'Ah, yes. Carole. Now, as you know, at this early stage it is quite impossible to make judgements about any child ...'

But you are going to, she thought.

'As Miss Arundel has told you, I am sure, the only way we can ascertain if the school is the right one for the child, is to see whether she is happy and productive. Now, would you say that was the case with Carole?'

Terry shifted in his seat, looked at her.

'She's only five ...' She was near tears.

'Are there any problems at home, bedwetting, rivalry with brothers and sisters? Anything we should know?'

'She had a hare-lip. Was operated on. But it didn't affect her.' Terry almost shouted at him.

'You think this is the reason for her – aggressive behaviour. She is aggressive, Miss Arundel?'

'Sometimes.'

'Has Carole had a session with our visiting therapist, Miss Arundel?'

'I thought she would settle down.'

'Why condemn a child of five?' Terry was belligerent. 'And if there is something wrong in the family, then why is Irene alright? It's the same background.'

'Now, come along, Mr ... er ... we are trying to find out what is right for Carole. Irene is a very bright girl. We hope for great things for Irene. We are not obsessed, however, with academic standards to the exclusion of everything else. I would like to keep Carole, but as things are, she really needs a special environment, more suited to her personality, her capabilities . . .'

'Thank you and goodnight,' Terry shouted at the empty schoolyard as they left. 'Special environment my arse. He means the scrap heap.'

'Anyway, it wouldn't be such a strain for her at a special school. She screams you know, every morning. She hates going . . .'

'It's too soon to tell.'

'*Terry.*'

'I'm off to the pub.'

The rain was spattering down. She'd left her umbrella in the classroom. She bought some chips for them, as she'd promised, and a bottle of light ale from the off-licence for Mrs Dawes, who had offered to baby-sit. The crazy opening of Bruckner's Seventh Symphony was pounding through her head. You are mad, my girl, she told herself, because it wasn't too bad, alone in the rain, popping the odd hot potato in to her mouth.

9

Once something had entered your mind it was caged in there as surely as you were caged in your own life. By rights she should have been sorting out the debris of a family – old comics, toys, do-it-yourself magazines, casting an eye over furniture that was falling apart after years of kid-battering. The old Broadwood piano, her gran's, would never go up to the high-rise, anyway, no one played it. Her gran used to knock out music hall songs, 'I'll take you home again, Kathleen' and 'My old man said follow the van, and don't dilly-dally on the way . . .' And here was her granddaughter, dillying and dallying like mad.

Stuck in the kitchen, Radio 3 blaring, she spent the mornings dreaming and smoking. Warren played at her feet. He followed his infant routine while she lost track of her adult one, such as it was. Symphonies, trios, quartets danced through her fuddled brain. She could do this until the end of her days, except Warren would grow up, and she'd be turfed out on the treadmill of part-time jobs.

One day she thought, why not? So she stuck Warren in his cot for a nap (hours early) and assembled a supply of rusks and some toys in case he didn't go off. She gave Pedro a huge plate of food, kicked the cat out, checked the gas jets and the ash trays, and buggered off.

The other two were safely in school until three. Freedom.

She got the train as if hypnotized. Raced through the concrete paths to the Festival Hall. Bought a black coffee and sat there, relaxed.

No knowing where Mrozek might be. Paris, Vienna, Rome. Enough of the feeling of him here to keep her happy. She stirred her coffee. She felt sophisticated, as if she too had somewhere to go. There weren't many people, a couple by the window, middle-aged, and, she guessed, in love. She didn't know how she knew that – it was around them like an aura. They seemed to avoid touching. He occasionally fingered his briefcase which was on the seat beside him. He should have been at the office. She had glasses and greyish hair, a tweed suit, good, but old-fashioned ear-rings, sensible shoes. When she smiled at him she had lipstick smeared on her big teeth.

O happy pair, she thought. What a bleeding mystery love is.

And suddenly, there he was. Not Mrozek, that chap who had driven them to Waterloo the day of the picnic. The drooping sandy moustache, the long hair.

'Hello. Mind if I join you?'

What could she say? He had been so kind, that other time.

'No,' she said. He was going to spoil her dreams of Mrozek. After all, she wasn't under too much of an obligation. Anyone would have done the same. Couldn't be rude, though. He was holding out his hand.

'Edward Rayburn. I'm a free-lance journalist. Actually, my lance is a bit rusty.'

She laughed politely. He offered to buy her a coffee.

'I ought to get back.'

He asked her if she worked around there. She said no, she was just passing.

'Passing time, like me . . .' He was supposed to be interviewing a musician, but his plane had been delayed.

'Who ?' she asked, heart in mouth.

'Jan Mrozek. Ever heard of him ?'

She nodded. Accepted his offer of a coffee.

'What are you doing here ?'

'Escaping from my life. Problems, you know . . .'

'You're too young and lovely to have problems. Cheers.'

Cheeky sod. Sending her up.

'Perhaps I can help with the problems ? Part of my job.'

'They are too – '

'Personal ? Nothing is too personal in the most impersonal of worlds.'

He did talk funny. He listened to himself all the time.

'I wasn't going to say personal. I was going to say boring.'

'Ah, Try me.'

'My house is being demolished – we have to move to a high-rise. I got a child who is backward . . . Terry's on short-time at the site.'

'My dear, you are the answer to a colour supplement's prayer.'

He got out a notebook. 'You help me, and I help you . . .'

'How ?'

'Mutual exploitation. You scratch my back and I'll scratch yours.' What on earth did he mean ? And what would Terry say ?

'Terry wouldn't like it. He's got his pride.'

'Terry being the husband ?'

'Terry being my husband.'

He didn't mind being put down by her. Unusual. The males she knew minded.

'Let me meet Terry.'

She jumped. That was impossible.

'I'm going. I left Warren on his own.'

'Was Warren the little guy in the push chair ?'

'That's right.'

He was one of those awful clinging types. She should never have accepted that lift.

'I left him in his cot – '

'Naughty naughty.'

She felt nasty but made the old excuse of the ladies'. She left him outsidc, by the telephones. If she stayed in there long enough, he'd get the point and leave. It was the old palais trick, leaving the spotty youths fuming outside until they got mad and left. She used to squeeze out of the loo window, with a friend. Speed off down the road tottering on high heels, giggling.

This wouldn't be so easy. She sat in the warm luxury, trying to pee. At lease she was connecting with Mrozek's drains. What a thought. How in hell's name could she get rid of Edward Rayburn?

'You O.K. in there, honey?' A blue-rinsed American voice. A coachload of elderly girls had arrived when she did, garish and noisy as a flock of birds. Some were here, powdering and preening, performing nature's functions.

She emerged shyly, knowing how long she'd been there. Washed her hands and dried them. She should not be here. At the pit of her stomach fear, of what Warren might be doing.

An American with eager glasses looked at her intently.

'Are you with our group? I didn't see you in the coach.'

'No, I'm not.'

'We just booked for Solti, Barenboim, Colin Davis and Mrozek. My, I'm so excited . . . Isn't it a thrill, girls?'

The girls made little noises of agreement. She felt like slapping the tanned made-up face. How dare it trip off his name like that.

'Jan Mrozek nearly took over the Cleveland – oh, I wish he had. He's *darling*.'

'I don't know anything about music. I just came in for a pee.'

She heard them clucking as the door shut. She slammed out into the waiting presence of Edward Rayburn.

'There you are at last. I took the opportunity of telephoning my editor. He thinks it a good idea. The high-rise business.'

'You're impossible.' Behind him she could see the Mrozek poster. Goodbye, Mrozek. And yet: Mahler's Third, Sunday, it announced . . . 'Lend me a pound?' she demanded.

He pulled out of his pocket one crumpled green note.

'It's my last. Treat it gently . . .'

'I'll pay you back from the family allowance. Where do you get the tickets?'

'Just over there. I'll do it for you. What concert?'

She told him. It was as easy as that. Seeing Mrozek.

He flourished the small green and white ticket at her. 'An admission to paradise. Hot pants for Mahler, like all the other ladies?'

'No, I . . . Don't tell Terry, if you ever meet him. He'd laugh.'

'He *wouldn't*.'

She looked in her purse to see if she had enough to pay his fare, as he'd given her his last pound. She had, but they'd have to hurry if she was to get the family allowance to pay him back. It was early closing day.

'Come on,' she cried. 'Run . . .'

He chased after her. Breathless. He seemed in bad nick.

The train said 'Mrozek – Mrozek – Mrozek' as it sped along.

Even if she didn't pluck up courage to go on Sunday, there would be her empty seat, no. 26*, watching Mrozek.

'What does the star mean, on the ticket?' He'd been dozing. That run had taken it out of him.

'End seat. End of row. Haven't you been to the Festival Hall before?'

'No.'

'Never?' He sighed. 'It's really been a most peculiar morning.'

She wondered what Terry would make of him, with his posh voice and dirty clothes. Wouldn't think he was having it off with her; he'd think him gay, most probably. The top half was sort of Spanish; a large black hat and an afghan waistcoat. The bottom half wore jeans and cowboy boots. He was very tall. The thing that would kill Terry – he carried a large handbag.

'You're admiring my tank-top,' he announced.

'Oh, that's right, yes. I can't quite read it . . .'

'*FUCK THE PIGS*. Dear Vanda did it. In fact that's why she's bunked off – she made such a success with her rude tank tops. She's been taken up by the big ones. Che Guevara, that bunch.'

She remembered his photograph, dead. He looked like Jesus.

'He looked like Jesus.'

'Not the man, dearie, the boutique. And she snaffled my car. Well, it was half hers.'

'He looked like Jesus.'

'You're right, he did.'

'What will you write about us?' She had become scared suddenly.

Edward rattled on about urban London; she thought of Mrozek. Her heart lifted. *Sunday*.

He hopped and loped beside her.

'Our readers, A and B, mainly, will be titillated. They approve of high-rise blocks as a solution to London's housing problem, without actually wanting to live in them personally. They deplore them as aesthetic objects . . .'

'You don't say.'

'But I do. Rather like motorways. Useful if one doesn't live beside one.'

'I'm afraid I'll have to get the kids first, before I get to the post office.' It would be closed now, anyway, but she thought she might borrow a pound from one of the Mums.

'Don't bother. I was joking about my last pound. See – ' He pulled out a fiver. 'So regard it as a loan, pay it back when you can. Or don't bother.'

'I will pay you back,' she said, reddening.

'Just as you like.'

She unlocked the door, watching Edward taking it all in, the squalor, the shabby hall, the stink of Pedro.

'Ugh.' Edward lifted his boot.

'Sorry – he is old. You'll find some kitchen roll by the sink. Take off your boots. I have to get Warren.'

Warren was bouncing around in his cot – he held out his arms to her. She hugged him tight. Edward, six inches smaller without his boots, stood behind her.

'Man,' said Warren, pointing a chubby finger.

'Right, old chap,' said Edward, shaking the little hand.

'I must take Pedro out and get the girls. Can you feed Warren for me if I stick him in his high chair?'

'I'll try.'

'Dad-dad-dad,' said Warren.

'Steady on – '

'There's some baby food, beef stew in a pan on the stove, heat it, taste it, and shove it down him. Small spoon . . . he's a good eater.' She hesitated. Didn't quite trust him. He knew.

'Look, it's alright. I'm an old hand at this. I had kids myself once. In another country, and besides . . .'

'Besides ?'

'Besides the wench is dead. A quote. She isn't really. She's in Australia. Which is as good as, really.'

'You're Australian ?'

'She is. And my children are I suppose. She married again. An old Australian family. An up-and-coming new dynasty. That's why I'm a dab hand at the baby dinners.'

She detected the sadness behind the bravado.

'Well, thanks.'

'I'll even change him for you. What more can a man do ?'

She dragged Pedro through the ruins, to the school gates. David Aspinall's mum accosted her.

'Who was the hippie ?'

'A friend of Terry's.

She and her companion tittered.

'Where's Warren ? Left him with the hippie ?'

Cows. She was sick of them. Nothing in their heads.

'*Still* coming for David ?'

'We're going to get some football gear. He's getting good. On the team.'

They boasted about nothing. But they all worked, bought their kids things.

'I hear you saw them about Carole. Any luck ?' said June Whitehead.

Irene appeared, holding Carole's hand.

'Give my love to the baby-sitter,' shouted Mary Aspinall.

'What baby-sitter, mum ?'

Irene wiped her nose on her sleeve.

'Don't do that. Take a tissue out of my pocket. It's that chap who drove us that day.'

'How did he know where we lived ?'

'I met him out shopping. He wants to do an article about us.'

'*Us* ? Why ? Will he take a picture ?'

'He might. I don't know. Don't say anything to your Dad, Irene.'

'Why, is it a secret ? Is he your boyfriend ?'

'No, silly. Now don't forget.'

'Is he looking after our Warren ?'

'He's giving him lunch.'

'But it's teatime.'

'Tea, then.'

She bent down and looked at Carole's face. Impassive as usual.

'She might get that 5p from the fairies tonight. Her tooth is nearly out,' said Irene.

Warren was staggering around, mush on his chin. Edward was in front of the television.

'Oh,' said Carole. She went over and touched his ringed hand.

'Hello, sweetie, want to watch ?'

She held her breath as Edward pulled Carole on to his knee. Carole didn't protest.

Irene leaned on the chair.

'I'm top of my class. Are you going to take pictures of us ?'

'No. I don't do the pictures. I might write something about you though. Do you like this ?'

'I'm too old for it.'

'I'm not,' Edward said.

'Have a fruit gum,' said Irene.

She tapped Edward on the shoulder.

'Sorry to disturb the viewing.'

He put Carole down, gently. Carole sat in his vacated place, pushing at her tooth with her finger.

They went into the kitchen, shutting the door because of nosey Irene.

'You'll have to go after tea. I'll make some bread and jam, and then . . .'

'I won't stay for the bread and jam, honestly. I finished up the beef stew. You're frightened of what Terry will say ? And yet you're not a conventional sort of girl, are you ?'

'No. Just wary. I had enough cracks made about you.'

'It's those working-class puritans. I saw her stare at us. Just jealous. Ashamed in front of your mates ?'

'Haven't any,' she said. 'But I wouldn't be.'

'Plucky with it. I would be. Ashamed of me. Ah, if I'd only been working-class. Who knows where I would be by now? All that energy thrusting up through the top soil from underneath. I've seen it – all those bright climbers, while I, blighted from the roots ...'

'Balls.'

'There you are – personality.'

'Anyone can say *balls.*'

'Not the way you did.'

He was a devious bastard. Clever with it.

'So it's goodbye, Edward?' She waited. Here it came.

'It wouldn't be possible for me to stay here, while I do the article?'

'Stay?'

'Rent your front room. You don't use it. I looked. I'm sure you could arrange it – you're a bright girl. Tell him I need to do it for the article.'

'He won't be over-joyed. Anyway, he's very jealous.'

'Tell him I'm queer. I don't mind.'

'He wouldn't have you in the house then.'

Irene peered round the door with saucer eyes.

'What are you doing, Mum?'

'Talking. Edward is going.'

'When can we have our bread and jam?'

'In a minute. Go on, back to the telly.'

'It's finished. Did you go to a school like ours?' she said to Edward.

'I went to school in the country. Well, not the country. Just outside London. Harrow.'

'Ha.'

'Your mum thinks I am a layabout, that's what the "ha" meant,' explained Edward. 'She thinks I should run the country, instead of watching television with you.'

'Damn right.'

Oh Mrozek, Mrozek. If you knew –

She piled doorstep-thick slices of bread and jam on to plates, carried them in.

When Terry came in she tried to hide the fact she was excited about something. And what was the secret – Edward, or Mrozek? The trouble was, Irene was bound to let the cat out of the bag, nicely, with her feminine instinct for delicate destruction.

Terry was exhausted; that was lucky. He'd been for a quick drink with brother Barrie. They always talked themselves silly. Terry was still close to his family. She resented hers, because she'd had to leave school. He never resented anything. Perhaps it would be better if he did.

There he was, sitting in the chair Edward had been in just an hour before, Warren in *his* lap, that was the only difference.

Carole never sat on Terry's knee. She was under the table now, a favourite place. Her tooth had come out; there was a bit of hysteria because Irene wanted to put it under the carpet for the fairies.

Later, in bed, she couldn't tackle Terry about the article. She wanted to ask him all sorts of things. About how he felt about *them* – whether life would always be like this. Whether he would mind Edward examining them, like insects, under a microscope.

'Want to talk?' she asked.

'I'd rather do something else.'

She turned away to her own side. The sagging mattress had a groove in the middle. That was the trouble, she always rolled back. She gritted her teeth and clung to the cold slopes. Gran's brass bed would have to go, like the piano; the size of modern rooms wouldn't take such oddities. They'd had some good fucks in it, too. Good job they had stuck it out in this bed, or they'd be parted now. For when all was said and done, it was another warm human next to you.

Terry tried to slip an arm under her, turn her over. She moved further away. Music flooded her head, a tune from an opera; a girl was receiving a silver rose . . . it was a lovely tune.

'No, Terry. For Christ's sake . . .'

He sighed, defeated, lying there in his ignorance. Dumb ox. He should hate her. He had a right to.

'Goodnight then, old love,' he said, her familiar back pressing into his chest.

'Don't you ever feel like hating me? I'm such a sow.'

'There's no reason to hate you.'

Oh yes Jesus, there is.

10 Edward

Two maxims for her: *One cannot live from anything except what one is.* And: *Error is just as important a condition of life's progress as truth.*

Both by Carl Gustave Jung. Of whom she may or may not have heard. Anyway, she would hear them with that wry smile of hers.

The day I saw her again in the Festival Hall cafeteria: it was one of those erotically damp October mornings. Slumped over the table, chin in hand, a coffee cup poised in her other hand, ready to sip, I thought she was reading a paper, but there was no paper. She was, I realize now, thinking of Mrozek. It was the quality of her stillness that attracted me. Peasant-like. One finds it in folk-art, though she is sharp, urban.

She hadn't expected to be approached by anybody. Least of all that annoying fellow who had insisted on driving her to Waterloo. I would venture to think she is uneasy with men of my type (whatever that may mean). Had great dignity in her surprise: reddening, pulling down her skirt slightly. It had ridden up exposing a delicate thigh. She was well able to cope with the situation. Looked at me with slight suspicion and curiosity. What could I want with the likes of her? It was written all over her face. Later she was cunning enough to try and lose me in the time-honoured way, in the ladies', hiding out for what seemed hours. I was persistent, and it paid off.

The thing which mystified me (and still does) was her sudden decision to ask me to lend her a pound, to get me to book the ticket. It had daring. I was intrigued enough to follow her home – to see how she functioned. When I learned she had left her youngest in the cot I was even more surprised. She is, above all else, a good mother. Her desperation: I wonder if she knows?

I decided to haunt this woman. After all, I've nothing better to do.

II

How she got away she would never know; that Sunday, the Sunday of the concert. It made her realize what a trap she was in, as she had never realized it before.

Terry didn't get back from the pub until one-forty-five. His dinner was stuck to the plate. He liked her to wait, and the whole family, for the ritual meat and two veg. (your Englishman's dream, wife and kiddies, the *News of the World*, a bellyful at the local, and then an afternoon snoozing in front of the box).

When he was done, she sprang it.

'I'm off then. Keep an eye on the kids.'

He hardly looked up. Had the grace, finally, to ask.

'I told you,' she said, 'this friend; in hospital. Visiting hours, three till five. St George's.'

There was a cake in the tin, and some orange squash on the 'fridge, for tea.

'You're all tarted up,' he said, taking his eyes off the paper for a moment.

'Not really. Just washed my hair, that's all.'

The lights of the Festival Hall shone out over the river. 'A typical Mahler congregation,' she heard someone say. They seemed young, though there were a sprinkling of women in furs and men in dark overcoats. The majority were girls with long hair and maxi-coats, and young men wearing ex-army gear and with hair as long as Edward's. An old man played the flute, by the bridge. She gave him 5p.

She felt a bit old-fashioned in her 'good' jersey suit Mrs Raphael had given her, when she worked for Mrs Raphael. She wasn't really much older than some of them so-called students who were flocking in. She was actually there, and not standing at the sink, up to the elbow in greasy roasting tins, listening to the echo from the football, and the squawking of her kids. She stood and drank it all in, trying not to look as if she'd never been there before.

The programme was a treasure she would keep. It had a description of Mahler's Third Symphony, and a biography of Mrozek. He was married, recently married, to a French actress. Her heart sank. She had never thought of him having an actual life.

She followed the crowds on and up; at each stage a new view of the river appeared. She felt nervous, as if she had to perform herself. She was shown her seat, looked down on the wooden platform, with all its seats for the orchestra, and empty rows behind, for the choir.

A few musicians ambled in, arranged their music, tuned-up. The audience rustled and gossiped, she looked around at them fiercely, as if she were in some holy place.

The man next to her read the programme. He sucked a peppermint. Cleared his throat.

Finally, a ripple of applause started. The man next to her jumped out of his skin, then joined in. She clapped too, though the man who had entered was not Mrozek. Suppose he was ill?

Mrozek walked out swiftly, to swelling applause, he bowed, turned to the orchestra and raised his baton. He waited. Everyone was silent. With one arm movement from him, it began. Music filled the hall. The music swept over her. It was enormous, the sound. Not like the radio. It carried you along like the sea.

He looked so stern, serious and pale. She would never dare, ever, to speak to such a creature.

She was swamped with the beauty of it. The female voice soared. The man next to her sniffed. And over it all, the magic hands of Mrozek, controlling. A mystery, a force. She wanted it to go on for ever. Just as it was getting too much to bear, it ended.

The audience went crazy. Released, as she was, from all that tension, they screamed themselves hoarse. The man next to her shouted 'Bravo', and then looked at her and smiled.

Against the sound, Mrozek, drained, weary. Making the chorus of small boys stand up, and then the orchestra. He was attentive to the soloist; he held her and presented her like a bouquet to the audience. They wouldn't let him go. He came back, and back again. She was so proud. He flicked a last smile over them, and left. They applauded, but he didn't return. He had gone. This time for good.

Was that it? Depleted, they were all going, stunned by the experience. Delighted, yet in despair, she pushed her way out too. Into the dark.

Students waited by the Artists' Entrance. She would have liked to do that too. There was no way of dispersing the emotions he had released. Now she had found this, how could she stand the rest of her life?

She didn't know what she wanted.

No, she knew what she wanted. That was much worse.

She heard footsteps. She hurried on. Who could know her, follow her?

It was Edward.

'Forgot where you were sitting. The usual Mahler chocolate ice cream. Didn't they go wild? Animals. Must you walk so fast?'

'Perhaps I'm trying to get away from you. Why did you come?'

'I was interested to see if you'd make it. Perhaps I'll blackmail you – secret assignations with the great composers. Next week, Beethoven?'

'Very funny.'

'While visions of sugar plums dance in your head? Have a coffee?'

He had broken the spell. She would never forgive him for that. She sipped the coffee, it burned her mouth.

'Recovered yet?' he said, gently for him.

'You do like to spoil things, don't you?'

'My dear girl, that was just an average performance of a Mahler work on a dreary Sunday afternoon.'

'You can't bear it – can you? The fact that I am –' (What? Fulfilled.)

'If you collaborate on the article, I might take you to Salzburg. How's that?'

'Don't laugh at me.'

'I'm not. People go to Salzburg all the time.'

'Not from where I'm sitting.'

'Widen your horizons . . .'

'Piss off.'

'I can't, you know. I haven't anywhere to sleep tonight. You know I said I was squatting ? Well, they threw us out. Take pity on me, you and hubby.'

'I don't call him hubby. Have you really nowhere to go ?'

'I'll be out there underneath the arches.'

'Are you really desperate ?'

He perked up.

'You'll do it ?'

'I think I can get you a key to one of the old pre-fabs that haven't been pulled down.'

He pouted.

'But I need a bit of human warmth. Your kids liked me. Especially Carole.'

She wished he would leave her alone. Mrozek would have gone away. She might have seen him but for this.

There was no way she could fight him and retain the memory of Mrozek. After all, what did it matter what she did if she couldn't have what she wanted ?

'I'll tell Terry. You get your things, and come along later tonight.'

'You're an angel. Just say I'm a friend of your friend who was sick in hospital.'

'How did you know about that ?'

'You told me, when we got the ticket.'

'And you remembered ?'

What a curious bird he was.

'What is your imaginary friend's name ? What about–Marie Helène ?'

'I wouldn't have a friend with a name like that.'

'That's the name of Mrozek's little friend. Or his wife, she is now.'

Cruel bastard.

'Oh, bugger off,' she said.

'I always get through to women that way – anger them. Part of my charm.'

'I don't find that funny. If you want to come, come. But leave me alone.'

The 'to women' bit annoyed her, she didn't know why. But worse than that, he had killed her pleasure. Was she never to have anything for herself alone ?

12

Edward had won. Over Terry, over her, over the children. Terry accepted the story. She'd arrived back all flushed and exhilarated and annoyed. He was glad to see her after the afternoon he'd had. Her story about Edward was accepted, no questions asked. He was quite interested about the article. Of course, he trusted her. Laziness or indifference? Perhaps she should have tried more things like this earlier. It was Edward's persistence, not hers.

At first he seemed a bit ashamed of Edward's accent – it was hard to take Edward down to the pub for a game of darts because of what his mates would say. Edward modified it, she noticed, when he was with Terry. No flies on him. He fitted in with the lads in no time at all. After all, that's what they learned in them posh schools, didn't they . . . to mix.

The trouble was to decide who Edward was conning. Himself perhaps. His financial contributions made a bit of difference, she was able to buy a few clothes for the kids. He helped out with meals, sloshing giant bottles of what he called plonk into everything, drinking the rest. It made a change. She didn't see much progress in the article; he told her journalists were stimulated by a deadline, they wrote worse when they had time. He didn't say if he had a deadline. The typewriter often pounded away in the front parlour, to all hours. Make them all famous, he would.

He was marvellous with Carole. He persevered with her – that was what she had needed. She tried, really tried, with Edward.

(Sometimes she wondered if Edward really knew things with such authority, or whether it was just that he had a voice with which they connected authority.)

She had no doubts when she saw Carole rush to him, hugging him around the knees, she who had never shown affection, and heard him greet her: hello, my pigeon.

This was the child who would never do much but sit in the corner, rocking, sucking her thumb.

'A funny sort of chap, though,' said Terry, one night when Edward was out.

Edward was out very little, and never brought friends back.

'What do you mean, funny . . . ? He's very good for us, and we may be good for him. He misses his family.'

'He could afford better elsewhere.'

'I don't know. Look at the way he dresses. Perhaps he pays lots of alimony. He did say she'd married again, though.'

'And there was I thinking he was queer.'

'Well, that wouldn't be unknown either, would it?'

'It's the handbag. I can't take the handbag.'

'Lots of men have them. It's just a fashion.'

'Wouldn't catch me with one. Does it make it nicer for you – that he isn't queer . . .'

'Would it make it nicer for you if he was?'

'Has a mother around, doesn't he? Rich? Why doesn't he visit her?'

Then Terry asked when this famous article was coming out.

'Journalists take months sometimes . . .'

'Fancies you, does he?'

'You know he doesn't. Wouldn't touch me with a bargepole.'

'Charming.'

'Well, you started it.'

'Fancy him though, don't you? Go on, admit it.' He was twisting her arm. Literally. She pulled away.

'As a matter of fact, I find him a bit sad.'

As a matter of fact he was someone to take away the loneliness. He told her when and where Mrozek was performing, all over the world. He'd even been to some of the places.

'What happens when we move?' asked Terry. 'Did His Majesty say whether he'll be coming with us?'

'Thought you liked him.'

'I do like him. I just don't fancy adopting him, that's all.'

13 Edward

Here in the room they allotted me, which years ago would have been the front parlour, and which does have a grand piano in pride of place, I squat, I write. Descriptions of them, their personalities, their artefacts, their habits. I want to suck the life out of them, for they are being stamped-out, by the concrete jungle, the commercial slime. They are city shrubs, soot-covered; they still endure.

My room has a Z bed, fitted in by the table. It's rickety, but I can type there if I put a wedge under one leg. I have a black Aladdin oil stove for heat; it goes furiously, sending out a warm pungent odour.

I wash in the kitchen, as they all do, with a diminishing cake of coarse soap which bears the imprint of dirty fingers. I dry myself on the communal roller towel by the back door, swivelling it round until I find a clean and/or dry section.

It is very damp, the parlour. The wallpaper bulges out into odd shapes. I lie on the camp bed at night; the street light outside makes frightening faces from the damp patches.

I feel like a child in the nursery again. I try to trace the feeling of comfort and security I have here. Does it come from her – or is it that I always like to be in a temporary situation – knowing as I do that soon it will end and this house, this road, this woman, and this existence will be wiped out – gone? I wonder.

In my more sentimental, or exalted moments I would go so far as to say that I have discovered some elemental truth – in my down moods I think I have just intruded rather dishonestly into some family's soul.

I have got back my childhood in this house.

One night I came into the kitchen. It was late. I had been copying out notes for my imaginary project – the article – and I felt great intimacy with them and was disturbed to see her sitting at the table, cradling the inevitable mug of instant coffee. She'd been crying. As I entered she wiped her eyes on the sleeve of her dressing gown. It didn't seem possible in any way to comfort her. I had to avoid that line, so hard to control, between empathy and a protective physical reaction very close to sexual melting. I wanted to help her, yet had to restrain myself from reaching out a hand to touch her. I was deliberately formal. I asked if she would mind if I took some milk; I gave her a boring description of my insomnia. She had been ready to spill out her life's anguish, knowing with her womanly intuition that I might have transcended my joking attitude.

I heated the milk in the pan she used for the baby, drinking it from Carole's Bugs Bunny mug. He leered at me, grinning through his front teeth. I scalded my mouth. I watched her collect her dignity and hand it to me on a plate, along with a ginger biscuit.

She crept off to bed, leaving me to contemplate my bravery, or cowardice, depending on which way I liked to survey her – or indeed, myself.

I decided then to do the article, rather as self-protection.

It was just that I was shit-scared.

14

Edward plastered the front room wall with posters – art nouveau, he said, and some old cinema ones, and one, for her really, of Mrozek.

He kept on to her about squatting in Camden – said he knew of a house. Semi-permanent, he said it was – they paid a token rent, so that would settle her Puritan conscience. She didn't bother to tell Terry. Terry was in work. Terry said the flats were not at all bad. Seemed likely they'd be settled soon, up in the sky. Without Edward.

Sometimes she thought Edward enjoyed her Mrozek fixation more than she did. There were days when she didn't have time to think about him. She said to him 'What's the use of it – dreaming of Mrozek?' and he said, 'Whatever turns you on love, don't knock it.' She felt better then, not such a fool. But the way she looked at it, really; it was beginning to diminish her.

When she bought the evening paper there was Mrozek waving goodbye from the airport, on the steps of the jet to New York. Off to conduct *Der Rosenkavalier* at the Met. Even the time was different there. He'd be in another world. She scrubbed the house through until it reeked of bleach. Terry complained and went out to the pub.

She bought a sketch book and tried drawing Warren when he was sleeping. She'd been good at drawing.

Irene told her this story about a Greek who rolled a stone up a mountain. As soon as it got to the top, it rolled down again. 'What did he do then?' she asked, not really caring. 'Why, he started rolling it up again, and again, and again . . .' Irene said. What a moron, she laughed. Why, that's no bloody Greek, she said, that's the story of my life . . .

She got the feeling then, laughing with Irene, that here was life – not far off in some concert hall. (Yet she still checked mentally what time it was in New York, throughout the day.)

The funny thing was, Edward seemed to know her, like Terry's dad did when he told her that poem. But no one ever *knew* anyone in that way. Not the family. Not Terry. She knew her kids that way; she was their mother. But they wouldn't ever know what she was – and she didn't think any man ever knew what any woman was. Of course she could be wrong on that. Wasn't Mrozek's attraction that she felt he 'knew' her?

She was easy enough to know. An extrovert, they all said at school. Got on with everybody. She wanted to embrace people as they walked along the street. That'll get you in trouble one day, my girl, her gran had warned. Far from it – it had no effect.

Men. If you tried to be over-eager, they thought you a slag. Women thought you were after their old man, or since Gay Lib., *them.* No one wanted all-embracing love. Women's Lib. thought men afraid of brain or competition. No, what a man feared was getting in too deep. Sometimes you could hug a child and it would move away fearing that you wanted to possess it. She had learned not to do this, with anyone; this was unnatural to her. That's why she had married Terry – at least he hadn't been afraid of emotion. He liked her dramatic attitude to life.

Suppose you had a god coming at you – like in Irene's book of myths?

Terry's body. Now too familiar. Always had some memories or rights over it. Never knew she would be the one to deny it pleasure; once had felt it an extension of herself, hated its tyranny, known its restrictions. Wouldn't willingly pass it over to someone else. (Would Miss Arundel like it?) Had soothed its aches, washed its coverings for years, yet had never, she thought, possessed it entirely, pleasured it completely, or belonged really to it.

Yet there had been times when such unison was created that it became more than marital or domestic affection, more than use. A cosmic feeling: it was like when you saw, for the first time, the earth from the moon. Strange, hanging there in space. Like letting go in heavy surf that time in Cornwall. But that was long ago in the history of their marriage.

Terry fucked and ran, now.

Terry, by his refusal to do anything that required effort, reduced their lives to garbage. Disposable.

In drink he and brother Barrie raged about politics, but they never bothered to vote. Terry behaved as if he lived on another planet, yet he'd been in Wandsworth all his life. He didn't live anywhere – the temporary man. Never raged against fate. Against her sometimes when she didn't deliver, but never against *them*. Whoever *they* were. Don't get upset. Terry's motto. Defeat. She hated him for his deafening silence in the face of everything. Stalemate. Stale mate.

In the blood, was it, the lethargy? His family, his old dad the same, much as she loved him. He had died quietly, after waiting two years for his hospital bed. 'Don't want to be no trouble.' He just wanted to be disposed of so as to be no trouble; removed neatly.

Bore it well, the family said, at the funeral. (All slippery pink ham and avoidance of the cancer. Stomach cancer.) Have another cup of tea?

He should have complained about his life, she screamed at them. They turned away, faces as pink as the ham.

Why should some hunks of flesh have it so good and others suffer? Thinking of Carole, thinking of Terry's dad. Why should the body she connected with spell defeat to her, while –

Stop, she told herself.

It should all be allowed, blood, guts, tears . . . Love. Isolation was the crime – *rage . . . rage . . .*

Even Carole' slip wasn't a defeat if you looked at it fair and square. Everyone wanted this world so comfortable, that was the sin.

She hated people's need for comfort. A bandage . . . 'How lucky hare-lips can be fixed up. Like new.' She wanted to say, if it was left to us, they wouldn't be. They'd still be there.

Why was it *they* never did the re-appraising, the repairing? When would they get to be the saviours of the world?

15 Edward

She has a fine vital face, still with traces of eagerness in the expression. Ruddy, slightly freckled with that chestnut to red hair Rossetti loved to paint; it hangs down girlishly when she is unaware or relaxed. Normally she restrains it with an elastic band into a sort of bun. A country girl by ancestry – her grandmother came from Kent – there is a bucolic quality about her when she isn't pushed into activity.

Slightly too stocky, the hips and belly bear witness to children, but the breasts and upper arms are superb. And the set of the head on the shoulders. Her legs are an indication of neglect, traced with blue veins. She wears the health clogs that are the fashion, and surprisingly her feet are perfect, like those on a Greek statue. I am hypnotized by the beauty of her feet.

Interesting to wonder what she would have been like born into a more leisured class; preserved slightly more than she is, educated slightly more than she is. Like many a hearty undergraduate of Lady Margaret Hall, I shouldn't wonder. Would she have gained or lost? Perhaps she would have lost something. Her validity is to be what she is, in her time. She would hate to hear this, I do know that much about her. Would hate to be told there is a sense in which she could only be the way she is. The earth under those feet is totally real.

(I have either treated her as an ethnic object, or as somebody with whom I am beginning to fall in love. I have never been able to polarize my relationship exactly with a woman. Until now.)

Terry is a Londoner through and through. Tough, shrewd but slow to react. A certain *machismo*, but this is overladen by the lethargy of his situation. A great lover of his children; not so much, I would say, of his wife. (*I may want to believe this.*) In early youth I can see what he had, and can see how he lost it. It isn't the century or the decade for Terry. The war would have given him an outlet; as it is he stews in impotence, and bullishly accepts what the Welfare State and his wife hand out to him. Feels diminished. Makes a feeble attempt to drown it in beer. Has a beer belly already. Looks me in the eye, thinks me (secretly) a poove. Envies my freedom, wonders how I got out of my marriage – yet without his family he would be diminished yet again. We play snooker and among his cronies he is relaxed and quite a wit.

He throws Warren up in the air and catches him and laughs, and for a moment one sees the real Terry.

Irene: shrewd, wary, father's eyes and mother's hair make a great beauty, but this is not what Irene is about. She has the bony translucence of the urban poor. Highly intelligent, and what is more important, as she will need it more, fanatically ambitious. She rarely asks anything that isn't relevant. Relevant to Irene. She won't be limited by the family, the mother has already recognized her potential, so have her teachers. She has a certain precocious sexuality, which she tries out on me with fixed and frightening confidence.

Carole: fair, plump, seemingly just a placid child until one hears one of her tantrums. It doesn't seem to be emotional deprivation. A slowness, resulting maybe from a hare-lip, though this shouldn't make any difference. There was a reluctance to speak which wasn't noticed early enough. A certain distaste can be felt from the rest of the family, although they would deny it. She has a dogged quality, Carole. Gets it from her mother. When she tries to understand what I am teaching her, her courage and persistence amaze me.

She has such quality of spirit, she responds to me with a trust that is touching.

(And if I have to leave her?)

Warren: a demanding masculine personality, as his father must have been before the world got to him. More forceful than the others, with a raging red-haired temper when he lets go. Can charm the birds from the trees, especially where his mother is concerned.

She, his mother, standing in the supermarket in the early morning wintry sun. Drooping, an Emily Brontë of the mail-order catalogue, patiently waiting her turn at the cash desk. Wearing a tatty fur coat, baggy scuffed boots, and a headscarf which slipped off as I watched.

(Not for nothing was I Women's Page editor for six months.) She moved the wire basket from arm to floor, and back again. Warren knocked over a pile of cans by the door and she picked them up, kneeling, after giving him a slap.

Followed her down the road. Her *private* private detective.

No one should get this intimate with strangers. My belly melted at her approach. Workmen whistled at her. She smiled when she was past them. The sun was shining, and for a moment she seemed to have forgotten Mrozek.

16

She woke and the world filled with his absence. Some mornings hopeful, others not. No reason for this.

Scrambling through the day, her feet and brain moving. No nearer, no further, dragging on to infinity. Another day filed in the dead cabinet.

Transistorized crackles attaching her to what now was reality, a gush of symphonic sound. And knowing she would never attain, never reach and never approach, never succumb, never be able to speak or express, never, apparently, have the means to, the opportunity to find a way towards . . . There was no possible way.

Torn fingernails, dirt-encrusted feet, open pores of nose and chin, greasy hair, eyes puffy with sleep, or lack of sleep. Figure swollen with carbohydrates. Could anyone desire, or rectify this mess?

Yet to have the guts to pull herself together, contract into a hard ball; and to hurl it (the you, the she), into whatever the object was. Marriage, childbirth, the lot. The body went on around this ball of defiance, dripping menstrual blood and shit, not real shit – duty shit, the shit the world dished out. She was surrounded by her own morality, self-sustained. A process not a person. The means by which others made their way, children flourished and functioned, men emptied themselves and filled themselves.

Anonymous, too. A dreadful word. Thought 'anon' was a real poet at school. DAZ FLASH OMO DETTOL BRILLO TAMPAX KOTEX COCA-

COLA HEINZ UNOX FINDUS BIRD'S EYE ... quite poetic too, like the poems of 'anon'. BIRD'S EYE, for instance, or SUNBLEST.

FIND US, BLESSED BY THE SUN, EYE OF THE BIRD ... sounded like a poem written by an Aztec.

Is that where the poetry lay, in the everyday, and not with Mrozek? Was life that simple? Eliminate desire and life is simple. The Buddhists believed it. She asked Edward should she be a Buddhist. My dear girl, he said, you are too much of a Catholic for that. He read her something better than 'anon'.

It said:

Whenever and wherever she appeared in the hope of receiving her miraculous salutation I felt I had not an enemy in the world. Indeed I glowed with a flame of charity which moved me to forgive all who had ever injured me; and if at that moment someone had asked me a question about anything, my only reply would have been 'Love' with a countenance clothed with humility. When she was on the point of bestowing her greeting, a spirit of love, destroying all the other spirits of the senses, drove away the frail spirits of vision and said: 'Go and pay homage to your Friend'; and Love himself remained in their place. Anyone wanting to behold Love could have done so then by watching the quivering of my eyes. And when this most gracious being actually bestowed the saving power of her salutation, I do not say that Love as an intermediary could dim for me such unendurable bliss but, almost by excess of sweetness, her influence was such that my body which was then utterly given over to her governance, often moved like a heavy inanimate object. So it is plain that in her greeting resided all my joy, which often exceeded and overflowed my capacity ...

Edward said, that's by Dante, about Beatrice, and that's what you feel for Mrozek, right?

And she said, yes, yes it was. And how the hell did he know?

17 Edward

The road jerry-built, Victorian. They always clustered them around gas works, a railway. Rows of terraces, now razed to the ground. A heap of rubble, and out of it rising like a phoenix, the new motorway.

No. 13, typical I suppose. A small front hall, vinyl-tiled (badly) by Terry, black and white with glue still caked between the cracks. The house reeking of cooking. The ghosts of meals past, present and to come. Seeped into the walls.

A grey folding push chair in the hall, obstructing access to the stairs. Beer and mineral bottles, returns, behind the front door. Dirty finger marks and childish graffiti cover the place. A door mat is stained by dog shit. On the door leading to the kitchen are children's heights marked in red crayon. Grey hair-cord goes up the stairs and on to the landing; it bears traces of dropped food and animal mistakes. Opposite the kitchen is the main living room. Pleasant, untidy, it looks out on to the back yard and gets the morning sun, which in turn illuminates the family possessions.

The rented television has pride of place. The family icon. The curtains are often drawn to shut out the sun, which obscures the picture.

A sagging studio couch which can only have been designed by a colour-blind manic-depressive is placed firmly opposite the set. Usually the whole family can be found there, sitting in uniform rapt complacency, eyes widening at the events constantly presented to them in black and white. The set needs attention, it overheats badly, and at times whizzes round like a mad merry-go-round. When I ask them about it they hush me, as they are usually watching something. They have a benign contempt for machines. Terry kicks the television to make it work. Sometimes they tell me they have rung the local branch of the rental firm from the call box down the road. I know this is untrue because the call box is unusable, vandalized.

Sometimes I wonder if it isn't their sublime oceanic indifference to everything that so fascinates and absorbs me.

Irene tells me her idea of heaven is a colour telly. I said it really wasn't that much better, and she said I had probably had one, and that's why I said it.

I was almost conned into inviting her back to my flat in Ebury Street. That would have been fatal.

A plaster image of a wire-haired terrier squats on top of the TV, oblivious of what goes on under its organ-less belly. One of those ornaments the middle classes have never understood, like the girl with the Borzoi, or the whistling lad, or the nodding dogs in the backs of cars. They don't have any purpose; yet they exist, loved objects.

I am usually offered a do-it-yourself rocking chair that Terry knocked together. It is a back-handed compliment, like offering me the damp front parlour for my own. Not done out of malice, but amusement, to see how I will take it. I have never seen anyone else sit in 'my' chair. I don't believe it was in use before I came.

She now puts the sugar in my tea before handing it to me, and stirs it, absentmindedly, as she does the children's. I find this a tremendous advance in intimacy.

They eat in the kitchen, but there is a big mahogany table, too large for the new flat, which is used for special occasions. It belonged to her grandmother. She doesn't seem to know the value of such pieces. They regard them, the brass bed, the piano and the table, as old-fashioned; would trade them in any day on some new stuff.

It's a fine thing to eat with them.

Sunday lunch is beatific, a tiny roast is surrounded by spuds, she usually makes a soggy Yorkshire pudding and soaks it in gravy. There are bright peas, frozen, it is true; perhaps an apple pie for which I have peeled the apples in the warm kitchen, throwing the peel over my shoulder to see who I am to marry. A feeling of conspiracy and joy with the smell of the roasting meat, and the cinnamon scented pie.

One Sunday we heard Mrozek conducting Mahler from Vienna. The Eighth. She found it marvellous, and burned the gravy.

Meals run permanently into other meals, the table is a debris of past events. No sooner is breakfast cleared than she has another cup of coffee and another . . . at least, it is a brown liquid, sometimes a dead tea-bag floats in it to give me a clue. If nothing is floating I presume it to be coffee. Then she feeds Warren, and before that is entirely over, the girls are back for bread and jam. Warren's toy cars are pushed aside, shop-bought jam tarts illuminate the table in jewelled reds, oranges and greens. The milk bottle remained since breakfast, cornflakes crunch underfoot. Pedro vacuums up some of the area, but he is too old and blind to see it all. To sit down is to risk the marks of spilled orange on the sleeve, squashed biscuit on the rear, or a chocolate thumb-print on the thigh.

I don't know of a better place to be in the evening, by the fire; the tea darkening in the mug, Irene reading, chin in hand, Carole on my knee, Warren running his cars through the sugar.

There's a calendar on the wall – a persian kitten of revolting sentimentality plays with a ball of coloured wool. The kitten has a deliberately cheeky expression, furry bum in air. The piece of silk ribbon which hangs the tiny calendar to the picture matches exactly the pink tongue of the pussy cat.

On the mantelpiece, a terrible bland clock *circa* 1938. It isn't working. A brass bell, a hand-tinted photograph of Terry's mum, a milk tooth, an ashtray full of buttons. A cork from a bottle of Spanish wine, a lethal school picture of Irene, a blue airmail letter from Auntie Dorothy in Hamilton, Ontario, Canada. A giant clothes peg with a barometer inserted into it, with the inscription 'A Present from the Lakes'. A letter from the headmaster of the primary school, saying Carole would be transferred to a Special school when a place was available. A blue plastic comb, with accompanying hairs, a dog collar.

These things have remained in the same place since I arrived. Everything is eternally fixed there, even the school letter. Occasionally I move it, to see if there is any effect from this. There never is.

The house at night, when they are asleep. Its bareness and integrity. The stale family smells. The spoor of an animal's lair. I shall miss the flap of a damp nappy in the face, the staggering gait of old Pedro – out to piss in the yard.

I contain them in my mind, and certainly in my heart. I breathe silently as I stand in the periphery of their being.

18

Her face, her flesh, with age added each day. She pressed her fingers over the skin, the hollows and dips and crevices as if it was already a skull. Familiar, unfamiliar.

She saw her children too as bunches of gestures, facial expressions. His ? Hers ? From an odd grandparent a muscularity of hand, a dexterity neither of them possessed, from an unknown source. A pursing of the lips, denied by them both as theirs. Warren's feet, a tiny repeat of Terry's. Made them laugh, one of Nature's jokes. Fudging the blueprint, distorting the pattern and then sticking in something identical. Does one realize, she thought, what a chance fuck puts in motion ?

She wept one day to realize that her genes and Mrozek's would never produce a pattern in the universe. Just as she had over Calum. (Calum had been a neighbour. Calum had died of leukaemia.) Coming out of the breakdown: on that occasion, she had wanted to die. Like Calum. She'd fought against destruction before that. A bird might flap over a cornfield, but need the mouse die ? Couldn't life remain calm, unspecial, without the quota of destruction – the extra sleeping pill, the fatal pregnancy, the torn womb, the induced miscarriage known as abortion, the gradual decay of some organ, the choking inhalation of vomit in the mysterious cavern of the lung ? Death in all forms haunted her after Calum. Then she started fighting again. It was necessary to defy.

A dream she had at this time: Mrozek's child. Carried in her belly to perfection. Like an explosion of composite joy. He came, bearing flowers, Calum/Mrozek, Mrozek/Calum. Then she woke.

She could hear the milk cart whirring on the wet road. It must have rained in the night.

19 Edward

I think of my own two blond sons out there in the Antipodes, rigidifying into people I may or may not like – who may not like me, but who nevertheless are fulfilling their dual mysterious genetic code.

They must act out her fantasies more than mine, after all, she won custody. God help them, in their stratified Sydney suburb. May they forgive me. And may they not appear, bronzed giants from Bondi beach, in a few years to condemn me in Freudian rage.

I could adopt Carole. It would do a lot for her. (And me.) But it wouldn't be allowed – they don't let flippant divorced males adopt little girls, and Terry would object – he'd knock my arrogant block off. It would help *her*, too. She might do something with her life. I manage Carole better and I have the cash. They don't know that, of course.

When I revisit Ebury Street it all seems so irrelevant; my Ciancimino table, my Bridget Rileys, which give me a migraine. How could I have conspicuously wasted so much? Earned as it was, loot from the Biafran situation, the Vietnam situation, or the plight of the inhabitants of Falls Road, Belfast. Such glossy reportage of suffering, such glossy rewards. But if I want to compare myself with colonizing forbears I don't make the grade as a full-blown shit. I guess I have exploited less for less. That doesn't make me a saint. No excuses. I can't do anything else. I need a reason for living as much as the next man.

Why is it I and my kind (and I don't mean class) would never put up with *their* existence, while envying its charms? We would have to tear out its roots. Boredom, or simple greed. The difference between me and Terry; give or take a few thousand pounds he would be the same fellow. Amiable, with a Ford Cortina, a semi-detached, membership of a golf club instead of his darts team. Basically the same. The old petit-bourgeois makes good syndrome. The tiny tottering steps of the British revolution. One by one, they may make it. I am more devious than that and so, I suspect, is she. I would prefer the way they live now to the Pinner nightmare. Would she? Terry would lose the best of himself in the exchange; at least he has a certain *machismo* now, all he would get from the other would be a mortgage and an ulcer.

Where does that little bit of reactionary passion get me?

Some of my best friends are drop-outs. Their indifference to the long-term (and short-term) plans of mice and men freezes my balls. They have never dropped far enough in to drop out. Politically any Italian peasant would run rings around them – and Terry. (I recall the dark printing shop which opened up on to the piazza in Arezzo – the posters rolling off, hot from the press – PER L'UNITA DI CLASSE NELLE NUOVE CONDIZIONI DELLA LOTTA POLITICA IN ITALIA.)

Why, oh why are they so passive here? I could knock their silly heads together.

One cannot deny that they, the family are in a sense victims. *But* . . . and in that 'but' lies the whole mystery.

Seeing her as an object. Do I do this with all women, or only her? Isn't this insulting?

My professed liberal conscience – a phony. I have a 'containing' role in this family, but I haven't been asked, have no official reason, I am no social worker, or therapist. I know more than I should, and interfere more than I've a right to do. I 'hold' her more surely than Terry because I can feed her information about Mrozek.

It isn't easy to look into her eyes. I feel shame. That isn't strictly true. I never feel shame.

But this woman is transparent – robust and cheerful sometimes, but with a dark feminine undercurrent – like the music in Don Giovanni. Mozart understood the dark menstrual edge of the female psyche; it cuts through the rococo like a knife. I recognize this in her; her cunning, devious, and finally defeated side.

I know in some ways I could save her but not in any of the ways she wishes to be saved.

I ask myself isn't this love of a kind I haven't experienced before, and, unable to answer that, I stew in my own frustrated juices. Am I a snob? Do I draw the line at her, physically, because of that? God knows, we have the opportunity – we stand in intimate conversation, face to face, eye to eye. Hers downcast, mine wide open to what I am doing, or avoiding. I feel a particular awareness at such moments, it is like being bathed in primaeval light. Any move, pressure of hand, intensity of gaze, would reveal me. I'm not ready to be revealed.

So I dare nothing. I draw back. Of course this feeling is entirely self-engendered and she may not notice it at all or want it brought to the surface. But don't all lovers fear this?

20

She waited outside Mrozek's house. She had sent the letter, the letter she had nursed in her pocket all those weeks. She had taken the bus and the tube, and there she was. She wondered why, for there was no point to it. All that had happened was that a Spanish or Italian housekeeper had come out and polished the letter box and bell push. She had moved a bay tree too, on the marble step.

A teachers' protest march had been coming along Park Lane as she travelled. It held up traffic, and generally annoyed people who wanted to get on with their own affairs. They made her feel a bit ashamed. Here she was standing outside some house, for some fantasy reason; and there they were, cheerful, shouting, with something to grouse about. But she didn't belong to them. If she had, then she wouldn't be here, clinging on to this. They were as remote from her as Mrozek.

It was embassy land, where she was. The large black cars, held up by the demonstration, slid past like fishes. It was bloody cold.

Flowers had been delivered earlier by van. The man who took them across winked at her. Had she told Edward the time to collect the girls from school? It all seemed so far away. She popped a Librium into her mouth.

At six she was rewarded by a glimpse of Mrozek. He dashed into the house, carrying a score. He looked different, he was in slacks and an Aran sweater. Back from rehearsal. There was a concert that night, she knew from the paper. She stared across, watched the lights go on upstairs. Changing for the concert.

Later, a blonde in evening dress stood on the steps. Marie-Helène? It was too dark to see. The car suddenly started to move. She could see them together in the back as it went past her.

The housekeeper clattered the bins in the area in front of the house. Threw out some old flowers. Her apron gleamed in the lamplight.

She walked over and poked into the empty area. The dustbins were many, and neat. One contained the dead flowers, some crumpled telegrams, and newspapers. On top, her screwed-up letter. She picked a few chrysanthemum petals off it and put it in her raincoat pocket.

The concert began at eight. She peeled Terry's spuds. There was a casserole cooking in the oven. It had been there all day. She was waiting for the magical radio link connecting her with Mrozek. *She'd seen him.*

She felt shame when faced with Marie-Helène – she could never catch up – not with all the lotions and beauty parlours in the whole wide world.

She yelled down the hall to Edward. Did he want beef stew? If she couldn't be Marie-Helène she might as well be kind.

Terry washed his hands in the sink before eating.

'Can't we have that bleeding row off?'

'No, I like it.' She turned up the radio.

He shoved the beef, mashed potatoes and cabbage down his gullet.

'Isn't it Bruckner's Seventh?' Edward said, fork poised.

That did it. Terry grabbed his jacket from the back of the chair, and slammed out.

'Good riddance. All the more for us,' she said, pouring out the tinned mandarins and cream.

Edward guessed that Terry was catching on. There was a conspiracy, and Terry couldn't put his finger on what it was.

As she washed up again, she thought of Mrozek, being driven back home in the rain.

21 Edward

I scavenged among their possessions like a derelict. For instance, when she was out I was up in the bedroom, their bedroom. They have a spectacular brass bed, a relic from the time when furniture had a beauty and craftsmanship that ceased with mass production. A stained sagging mattress lies on it – it doesn't fit. This gives the place its vulnerable quality: the crane will probably swing in when she has just washed the kitchen floor. It doesn't deter her, she goes on. If she stopped she would lose her reason for existence. What a waste of energy anyway. It should have a better use.

The bed shines. A gleaming ship of pleasure, I'm sure it was once. Is no longer.

A cheap looking-glass which elongates the figure has the tiny footprints of a winter fly. A chest of drawers, with the rings of glasses and cups and the brown cigarette marks of smouldering fags (Terry smokes in bed), bears her collection of pots and jars of cream, all corroded around the lid. She doesn't bother to cream her face at night. Irene's black crayon is sometimes used to outline her eyes, a worn lipstick lies next to a jar of Librium. She is careless, the kids could reach them. I toy for a minute with the idea of removing them, then decide not to. Terry's side of the chest bears a nylon hairbrush, with his dark curly remnants in it: a can of deodorant, a jar of hair-cream.

The top drawer: hers. Two underslips, flowered black and orange, with matching pants, three pairs of nylon briefs (stretch variety). Two bras. One white cotton, with a safety pin in the strap, one a wired undercup Jayne Mansfield type which she hasn't ever worn to my knowledge – I'd have noticed. 36B. One pack of Kotex, half-empty. Two scarves. Four wire hair rollers, violent pink. A tube of antiseptic cream, a cup with a broken handle, loose beads all in a jumble. Two nail files. A small teddy bear. Transparent nail varnish. A final demand for the gas bill. Three tampons. The drawer is lined with the Sunday Mirror July 2, 1972, and under this are hidden cuttings from newspapers. All these cuttings feature Jan Mrozek. One is a photograph of him rehearsing a soprano in the part of Zerlina. One is Mrozek at the airport, arm suspended in farewell. The last a shot of him and Marie-Helène at a first night – Marie-Helène's eyes have been scrubbed out with eyebrow pencil.

Terry's drawer: a pair of nylon pyjamas, garish blue; the other pair are on the line in the yard. Those are red. Two white cotton shirts with a permanent greasy neck and cuffs. One pink-and-white striped shirt, collar 15½. Terry has a bullish but not large neck. One darned sweater, grey lambswool, one T-shirt (olive green) one towelling sports shirt with a dragon on the chest pocket. One pair of navy swim trunks, edged in white. Assorted socks rolled in balls. One odd one, stiff with frequent washings. Two dark-blue vests with sleeves, matching dark-blue briefs. Hey, they are just like mine. Two pairs of Y fronts, white, one with a hole in the crotch. A pair of cheap cuff links. Two packets of Gossamer Cloud Durex, one unopened, the other containing two condoms. An assortment of nails, screws, and a yellow perspex handled screwdriver. Two 15-amp plugs. A golf ball. Two white (grey) handkerchiefs. Three ties, two are polyester, one striped, one bright red. The third is a green silk one. Under the newspaper, an old thumbed *Mayfair*.

The two bottom drawers pay homage to the life of the family. Old snapshots, childrens' tights, hair ribbons, biros, a chocolate box with a picture of Buckingham Palace on the lid. It contains buttons, of all colours shapes and sizes, darning wool, cottons, needles, pins, a blunt pair of scissors (no good for toe-nails), every kind of material.

Also: childrens' drawings, all marked with name and date, and to me, all exactly the same. Pin people, square people. Stick people.

The wardrobe smells of moth balls and sweat. A tatty fun fur and a navy blue overcoat (male) hang in a zipped plastic bag. Various dresses, from size 12 to 14 hang limply, swaying. She seems to hang up sweaters too, which explains a curious bulge I notice on the sleeves.

A grey flannel suit which I've never seen on Terry bears his figure without him. The trousers have concertina thighs. It must be for special occasions. They haven't had any since I have been here.

A straw summer handbag gives off that lovely stink of beach oil and sun.

Shoes mysteriously contain the personality of the wearer. Seeing them together, a masculine and feminine pair, leaning against each other in intimate collusion gives me a pang of marital envy. Symbol of a run-down marriage. Her stilettos leaning over the brogues. I feel pity, tenderness, jealousy in that order.

What poverty has joined together, let no man put asunder.

Warren is also in there, with his cot with the dancing lambs on each side, his pottie, and his familiar constant smell of piss. The bathroom, unused. Cases and boxes are stored in here. They have gone green. The window is cracked and mended with Sellotape. The bath, rust-stained, had been used for washing; an old clothes horse remains straddled across it, bearing a forgotten towel.

The last room, smartly vinyl-floored and wallpapered, is the girls' room. Bunk beds take up most of the space, there is just room for a tiny dressing table, kidney shaped, with a chintz skirt. Irene sleeps in the upper bunk, Carole in the lower.

On the chair which is Irene's: a pair of blue jeans, a pair of dirty gym shoes. An ornamental plastic hair slide. A copy of David Copperfield (school reader).

On the dressing table (more a desk, really): A tin of all-purpose cream (which she rubs on her knees and elbows, she is a tomboy), a clean fresh notebook, with 'My Diary' written on the front. A fountain pen, ink. Homework, all done, oh ambitious girl. An alarm clock ticks away with Noddy and Big Ears.

Her bed: a jumble. A cotton nightie exuding her little-girl smell of toilet soap and sweets. Her quilted dressing gown bears the traces of early-morning egg.

Carole's bed: a boat in which she voyages, rocking. Sucking her finger. Her dolls, line against the bottom of the bed. Repulsive sexually-aware dolls, with wardrobes and careers, with dyed hair and expensive clothes. Bought to make up for something, obviously. Such costly toys. Carole makes noises to them and often hurls them across the room.

I once tried with Carole and the dolls the old con game of calling one mummy and one daddy; then watching and waiting. She either forgot which doll was which, or she is the best-adjusted child I ever met. She ended each test by trying to say 'Edward', and to hug me, which wasn't the result I wanted.

She and I have discussed Carole, she feels the blame for not trying to do something. Deeper than that, there is a fear that during the pregnancy she was disloyal. She kept having dreams about a boy she knew, who died, Calum. Women have mysteries about such things – explanations of fatal occurrences, touching in their revelations. It was as if she thought her (erotic ?) memories had in some way marred the child in her womb.

I found out that she had destroyed her future for Calum. She had been a bright Grammar school student, and when she found out he was dying, it wrecked her. She stayed off, finally left school. Her mother sent her to work in the local shoe shop.

Not only was Carole her reminder of the loss of Calum, but also of her own non-functioning. Her former self was haunting her.

She didn't want this dragged out in the open. She treated me formally for a while, a deadly insult in her book. She practised against me that subtle torture hurt women use against those who have prised them open, letting air into their wounds.

When she did talk to me she said what frightened her was the great ocean of the incomprehensible – only she didn't put it like that. She said she stretched out her arms to something which was, she was aware, unknowable.

If the world had not been out of true, had been straight, the thing would be there, knowable, for all.

Wasn't that why women felt disappointed, she asked? She considered becoming a Catholic, because it seemed to her the Catholics were on to it. More than others, anyway.

The only intimation she had got of this mystic thing she had got from Mrozek. And so at last I understood her obsession.

The ridiculous thing: she doesn't believe *they* are *real.*

And me? I will creep along to Ebury Street, I suppose, having given her my attention, my love and perhaps a record. Mrozek conducting – what? Beethoven . . . Missa Solemnis? She'll get more out of it than I would, for I was taught to handle Beethoven with sugar tongs.

22

Christmas took it all off, the obsession. She was almost her old self again. Almost.

Edward was going home for Christmas. Home, meaning his mother's place in Suffolk. His mama he called her. Frightened of her, his own mother, she could tell. How could a son be afraid of his mother? She asked him what his mama was like. Brittle, he said. Does that mean breakable, delicate? He said he meant, rather, that she'd been mended in many places, like fine china, with wire clips.

'What kind of a Christmas do you have?' she asked.

'A country one. Midnight service in the village church, sometimes a few people in for drinks.'

'At midnight? No stocking?'

'At midnight. I never had a stocking. I got my presents at breakfast. Late. My mother liked to sleep late.'

She decided they would make him a stocking to take with him.

How sad, she thought, thinking of the white, red-paper trimmed net stockings, with tangerines and chocolate mice, and the cheap toys which didn't last out the day.

'What do you get for your mother?'

'She only trusts her own taste. But she likes historical novels, or memoirs, and if she has read them she can change them if I get them at Harrods – she has an account.'

'What does she give you?'

'Commercial after-shave she has seen advertised on TV. Underwear. Or nothing at all.'

She never knew when Edward was teasing her.

For instance, one day he said, 'You have a face like an unmade bed.' She was so hurt she almost cried (she hadn't slept much, Warren had a cold). He said, 'Hey, it's a compliment, stupid.' And rushed out. He even left his goat coat in the hall, and wasn't back all day. When he did return he had a record for her. Mahler songs, his first work. He told her to listen carefully, as it was an indication of all that would come later. Said the unmade bed remark was a sign that he –

Warren howled at that point and he never finished what he was going to say.

Edward and Terry got on. Formal, like men are, snooker and such. Christmas eve, Terry was out getting the turkey, Edward had wanted to go with him, but had stayed too long having Christmas drinks with his friends at El Vino's.

He drank a quick cup of instant coffee in the kitchen before leaving to get the train for Suffolk: it seemed to her he was near to tears. She'd never seen a man cry, not even Terry when Carole was brought to him. He held it back. Well, Terry would.

Perhaps Edward didn't want to go, though it sounded lovely. Orford. She said why don't you stay, if it is going to be tough – but perhaps you should see your old mum. He laughed at that. He said he just felt a bit down, had a cold.

She felt like saying, cry if you must, but don't pretend it is just a bleeding cold. Christmas affects some people that way, they get depressed.

He'd been taught to hate showing his feelings. He found it hard to be straightforward, that's why he came out with the jokes so often. He once said to her, if I was honest with you, you'd have to watch out for me. She didn't know what he was getting at.

When she went upstairs she discovered a huge green bag from Hamley's. Inside were the presents he had bought for them; a dragon puppet for Carole, a large Snoopy dog for Warren, and, best of all, for Irene, a pair of white boots and skates, like the top skaters had. It was her turn to shed a tear. Where had Edward found the money for such things? And him only a free-lance, with not much work on. There was a bottle of red wine for their Christmas dinner. She felt ashamed they hadn't given him anything, except cards the kids had drawn, and that bulky silly stocking packed with razor refills for his techmatic, and some cigarettes and a Penguin book by Fanon called *The Wretched of the Earth*, because that is the kind of thing he liked to read, though it didn't sound very holiday-like, but she'd seen it, and he'd once mentioned it to her.

Irene was desperate to try out the skates, so as soon as the rink opened at Richmond, they were all there.

They hired skates, even tiny ones for Warren. He fell about, a padded bundle in his anorak, making people laugh. And knew it, little devil.

Irene got the hang of it immediately. Of course she'd been an avid watcher of the skating on television. She went round the barrier two or three times, doggedly, ankles sagging. Her chin took on that determined look, especially when she saw the other girls weaving and skimming over the white surface, twitching their little behinds in their short skirts – attempting spins and jumps. By the time mid-morning came, Irene was stumbling out towards the centre of the ice. Her ankles were straight.

She and Carole plodded around, ankles weak, nerves more so. They didn't like to let go of the barrier. She looked at Carole's tight little face – why couldn't she have been the one to take to it? Warren was with his dad, being pushed around. Terry was the big surprise. He had done some ice-hockey skating once, played for a scratch team. He'd never said. It was odd, finding he had a skill she didn't know about. He was, after the first few awkward minutes, a graceful skater. Slow, full of confidence. He skated like he made love.

He was a very physical person who was never allowed to show it.

Carole and she retired to the snack bar and ate hot sausage rolls. Carole's ankles were aching, so were hers. It was pleasant here, but what had it got to do with anything? With her? With *Mrozek*? It was for Irene.

Warren's rosy face beamed at her, as he whizzed by, held aloft by Terry. People went round and round, multi-coloured, as if on a revolving stage. She saw Irene, trying hard.

So Edward had known that; Irene needed something to work towards. Bless Edward for making it happen.

What would Mrozek be doing? Perhaps in his Swiss chalet, like she had seen on TV? Sitting in the sun on a balcony, studying scores. Or perhaps not relaxing at all, but rehearsing in some bare hall, music flowing out as it had that day . . .

She said to Carole, come on, we can't let that lot beat us.

The ice was like glass beneath them and they clung together as if drowning. It was worse if you had come off and gone back. Carole began to howl, people started looking at them. She took her off. Sat behind the barrier and watched the others. She herself had never been that good with physical things – didn't ever get to the point where they became easier. The place here was fine, cold, with an ammoniac smell; and the sound of blades cutting the ice; young boys slicing up the ice on hockey skates, tittering girls with dyed hair, chewing gum, who tottered around as if they were in Oxford Street. The odd mum gliding with an infant, the old graceful ones, doing it for the exercise, and the star turns. It was like a picture in a child's book – or like that description she had once read at school, of people in olden days, skating on the Thames.

A young man with a checked shirt weaved through the crowd. Moving fast, he seemed about to perform some feat. After two rounds of the rink he suddenly lifted in to the air in a split jump – for a moment he was suspended in mid-air. Slow motion, as in a dream. He landed perfectly, grinned, and did it all over again. This time he spun three times in the air, and landed. His friends gave him some mocking applause. Suddenly she was reminded of Mrozek, and it was all ruined.

Mrozek ruined everything. Why did perfection upset her so much? Why, with people enjoying themselves, the music beating out a sense of excitement and joy, did the sense of loss have to strike her? She took Carole in the snack bar again. Watched her paddling her fingers in the spilled tea.

She could see that this would become another family ritual. Every Sunday they would want to come here, all except Carole. She had the choice, to sit here watching the world glide by, or stay at home with Carole, feeling left out.

It was just another nowhere for her. A place where he was not.

She pressed her lips to the back of Carole's warm animal neck. If only Carole would communicate, she would . . . what? Give up the dreams or Mrozek?

Why should she? It was all she had. She rubbed her shin – even that was a memory of meeting Edward, and not *him*.

She hated the obsession which made her unfaithful to all of them. It twisted up her insides, made her abstracted, dead. It couldn't be the thing she had always searched for, needed. Because if that were the case she would be happy. Not bloody miserable. Unless that was what a revelation was! a knowledge of impossibility.

Irene wobbled off the ice.

'Ready to go home? You did very well for your first time.'

'I like it, mum. I want to come all the time. Get good at it. I want to get a gold in the Olympics.'

'I thought you would. Let me untie your skates.'

23 Edward

Mother was putting on her face for the Major. She never gives up. I do respect it – the iron will of the upper-middle-class Englishwoman. I have seen her devastated by illness, marriage, the tiny relentless steps of age; I have never seen her go under. As a small boy I hated this veneer; as I grow older I admire her more and more. That is what she has settled for.

Two of her husbands left her for love. My own father for the love of a barmaid from Brixton. Let's hope he hasn't the nerve to bring her to the Eton–Harrow match, mother had said. He had.

I used to visit them in their pub. Mother never knew. Is that where I got my sneaking admiration for working-class warmth? Am I chasing the bawdy romantic image of my father's elegant hand on a barmaid's behind?

Mother's Christmases are animated by large amounts of criticism. Before I got inside she had said I dressed badly 'even for a journalist', and that she had better hang my afghan away from where the Major usually put his raincoat.

The Major. He watched her like a hawk as she swished around the drawing room from drinks cabinet to TV cabinet and back. The television was elaborate, with folding doors, so that one could pretend one hadn't succumbed to the vice. I had a sudden vision of *my* family in Wandsworth, lined up on the tartan couch, munching crisps and sweets, trying to shove Pedro on to the floor, so as to have more room.

My companions became sedately tight. The Major drifted off finally into a snoring agitated doze. She lifted the glass from his hand, gently.

I made the mistake of asking mother if she thought responsibility was an essential part of love. She always warmed to pseudo-philosophical conversations after dinner, but this time she seemed alarmed. Perhaps she thought I was going to drag out my childhood again. She rushed around, emptying ashtrays, re-filling my glass. You aren't feeling responsible for anyone, are you? she asked. I said no, I wasn't feeling responsible for anybody at all.

We walked the dogs to the castle and back in the rain. She told me she hated old age. I told her she hadn't aged; untrue, it has suddenly hit her, like a ghost, under the transparent umbrella. You are tough, I said to cheer her. Tough she had never wanted, tough wasn't nice.

I mean it in the Hemingway sense, grace under pressure, I told her. She replied she'd met him once in Paris, dear Ernest, and – but, my father . . . I asked if she would be happy with the Major? She said she would arrange to be. I kissed her on her wet cheek. She stared at me. Told me not to mess up my life as my father had. The witch. Could analyse me any day. Clever lady.

Come Solomon, come Sheba, she shouted, over the cold wind from Orford Ness. Let's go in.

Bedded down after driving the Major a few hundred yards (hoping their modesty was not for my benefit) I listened to the wind howl over the marshes. If she had been a more conventional mum I might now be in a haven of nostalgia, with photographs of defunct cricket teams, certificates of music grades framed on the wall, thumbed copies of Henty. As it was the room was as impersonal as any of the rented houses of my childhood, classy and formal, with a copy of a new American bestseller by the bed. In any case, I was not in the cricket team. I failed my music examinations. I was just as unsatisfactory a son as she was a mother.

Christmas over, they insisted on driving me back to London, though I insisted they need not bother. Mother complained the place was like a morgue – said I should get Mrs Etherton, the housekeeper, to look in more often. As I had not been near the place for weeks, I was terrified they would meet. The fridge stank – there was a decaying steak and a lemon in there. From the sitting room I heard her cry out that there was no booze.

The noble Major went out and reappeared with three little boxes of chicken, and three bottles of light ale. We sat on my hide sofa and ate solemnly, wiping our fingers afterwards on the impregnated cloths provided. That sort of thing depressed her. The Major was in for a bad return journey. He could at least have got a bottle of decent wine, she grumbled, as he went to the bathroom to do a piss. Sometimes I despair, she said. I told her to be kind to him. He had at least gone out for food.

She raised her pencilled Garbo brows, and shrugged. It did not augur well for the future, I thought.

I went down with them and tucked her in, fixed her seat belt. Put my head in and kissed her good-bye. She put a cheque in my pocket. At least, I thought it was a cheque; she often used to do that as we parted. When I looked at it, it said: 'Darling, I've got cancer. Not the worst kind . . . so not to worry. Don't tell him.' I didn't know if the 'him' applied to my father, or to the stolid silent Major. I stuffed the note into my pocket. It burned against my hip.

I wanted to get back. *There*. I should stay here and forget about them, my family. Have her up here for a few weeks, poor brave mama . . . Instead I got on to the old Southern Region, heart pounding.

There was no one in. I couldn't believe it. The familiar smell, old fat and damp, met me. Pedro gave me a welcome. In the kitchen the kettle still retained some heat; they must have just gone. I was anguished. More than at the thought of my mother's cancer. I brewed some tea in the brown pot, sat down next to Pedro on the couch. He groaned and moved over. I was lost. I waited, they did not come. They were *never* out, not in school holidays. I turned on the box – an earnest actress told me a story. Then I saw a children's adventure serial. I poured some tea in a saucer for Pedro and held it for him. He looked at me with adoration. His beard dripped on me as he drank.

The house charmed and horrified me. I was taken over by this dim place, this slum. Had I allowed it to happen – that this should now be the only possible place for me to breathe in ? I missed them. I did more than miss them. I couldn't conceive of not seeing them, always having them in my vision. But they were not mine.

My mounting anger at their absence which I took as some ridiculous betrayal (how dare they not be there) was almost enough to make me come to my senses and leave. Instead I washed the lunch things; plates with congealed traces of fish fingers and tomato ketchup, mugs of milk and coffee, my own cup and Pedro's saucer. Pedro's plodding form followed me as I mooned about the house, finally flopping down on my cold hard bed. The agony of waiting was so intense I shut my eyes to wipe out the world until she should come.

A tap on the door woke me.

Carole rushed in, shouting, Edward. Blurred, but Edward it was.

She looked in, Warren on her hip.

'We went to Snow White,' she said. 'Oh ... and thanks for those things. Particularly the skates. You shouldn't have – really ...'

She was maladroit, always, at thanks and compliments. Given or received. Asked me about Christmas, hiding a little behind Warren. I think she was glad to see me. I stuttered and stammered, stunned with sleep. She called Irene to come and thank me. Had I had some tea?

I said yes, I had.

Carole loved the puppet. I could see her work it later.

Leave Edward alone now, she said to them, ushering them out. Closing the door.

I sank back on the bed. I had something for her – a review of a Mrozek performance, but it could wait.

I was home.

24

Edward was back.

He had brought her a Mrozek review.

JANACEK TRIUMPH AT COVENT GARDEN

With the high musical standard we have come to expect from his concert performances, Jan Mrozek last night made his debut at the Royal Opera House with a superb performance of Janacek's The Cunning Little Vixen. The opera, little known in England, is new to Covent Garden, though Glyndebourne did a highly successful production two years ago. The cast sing in the original Czech, and Ludmila Halir, from Prague, singing the role of the vixen, is a delight. I look forward to her Susannah, also with Mrozek, later in the season. But the laurels belong to the orchestra, who particularly in the strings section respond lovingly to this new relationship with the Polish maestro.

Malcolm Mudd.

'What would you like, light ale or anything?' Terry was slicking hair over his balding patch at the sink. Off to the pub.

'Nothing thanks.'

'Bloody misery. On the pills again?'

Terry thought it was morbid, cushioning yourself, but was the whole world cushioned, then? And if it was, perhaps that was the way it was. He thinks the new place will make a difference, but she knew better. Look at the faces, she told him.

Life keeps dragging me down, she used to say to Terry – now she said it to Edward. At least Edward agreed, where Terry always blamed her. He was so institutionalized, that's what Edward said it was when you didn't know how you was being pushed.

'Come on. It would cheer you up to see Barrie and Jackie.'

'You must be joking.'

'I'm off then.'

'I'm not stopping you,' she said. The idiot thought she cared. Damn him, he knew her no better than the day they met.

The Eroica was on. She sewed a skating skirt of lovely material she picked up in the market, for Irene. You didn't need much material, they were tiny little things. She would look lovely, gliding around the ice in this, with a red sweater. She had a chat to one of the instructors there, at the rink, and he said she had real talent. They arranged for him to teach Irene. She could get a job at the laundry and that would cover it.

Terry might object to her working, but to hell with him.

She asked Irene how it felt, being good at something. She asked her what she felt when she did one of those little jumps (she could, already) did she feel marvellous, in control, all that? Irene said it was never quite good enough. Then you tried to do it better – each time was different.

And she thought, *that's it*, she's got the idea.

'Why don't you do something, Mum? I mean, you do my skirt, and you could be a designer or something. Why not become a skating-clothes designer?'

'Do they have such things?'

'They would. You could be the first.'

Oh, kids.

'Here, try this on.'

Irene stood on the table. It just needed taking up a bit more.

'You weren't bad-looking, were you, Mum?'

'Suppose not.' Her mouth was full of pins. 'Stand still.'

'Edward fancies you.'

She felt herself go red.

'Don't talk nonsense.'

She slapped Irene's thin behind with affection. Lifted her down.

The Eroica finished. She went to pot Warren. Traces of mould in the bathroom seemed better since Edward had been living underneath. Ironic, that was. Warren swayed on his pottie. She picked him up and said he was a good boy. He gave her a filthy look through his half-closed eyes. Exactly like your dad, she murmured. She hummed him a bit of the symphony as she tucked him in. Pulled the curtains closer together – those bloody red-and-brown leaves entwined; they'd even had them in their first room. She'd stamp on them and tear them up when they left. She'd counted the leaves while sweating out the brats. Forty-seven from ceiling to floor, in rows of twenty. Turned into little evil grinning faces they did, when you squinted at them.

She liked it when Terry and Edward were out, she felt more herself; not just to think about Mrozek, it was just that when they were out she wasn't put in a category. Free.

25 Edward

I said to her, would you let me study your body, objectively, as a doctor or painter would, it's for my work – and she looked at me with canny knowingness as arrogant as ever, and said: 'Want to bet?'

But then slowly and with great dignity she first removed her blouse, revealing her upper arms and bosom, apricot coloured they were, the apricot blending into peach.

She went over then and locked the kitchen door, her blue eyes full of mischief. She had me transfixed, and was enjoying it. She moved over to the kitchen chair and sitting astride it let her bosom free from the white cotton bra, size 36B, and her flesh was ripe but firm, her breasts must have been marvellous before children; now they were heavy but still beautiful, oval and pink-nippled (I suddenly remembered my girlfriend Anya's banana breasts; these in comparison were strawberries-and-cream).

She undid the hooks of her skirt, and stood there for a moment in her cotton briefs, thighs like columns spread apart. Then she lifted one leg, then the other, and stepped out of the briefs. Her belly was large, a gourd. Legacy of those three. The dark hairs were profuse, extending from her cunt almost to her navel. Her torso was thick, but shaped.

Her legs, when released from the cutting line of a skirt, were perfect. Her delicate feet were as statue-like as before.

'Seen enough?' Revolved before me, mocking.

Her buttocks were slim and sloped down, her back shapely, her neck was getting the middle-aged droop. I wanted to go over and bury my face in her ample belly.

It was inconceivable that she did not sense the depth of my emotion.

'Jesus . . .' I muttered.

She dressed slowly. A child rattled the door handle.

'What were you expecting, Raquel Welch?' she said, bitterly.

'You're not so bad,' I said. (God in heaven, what had I done?)

26

Down at the market, on Saturday, Irene and her friend Isobel sold some clothes, twenties and thirties stuff mainly, which Isobel's aunt had let them have for dressing-up. Isobel had asked her sister, who worked in television wardrobe, if the stuff was saleable – and they made a bomb, flogging them. Thirty pounds. Business acumen you could call it. All good stuff, satin evening dresses, feather-trimmed. They'd done it so that Irene could go on the school trip, Isobel said. Isobel came from the other part of Wandsworth – her dad was an architect. Irene hadn't asked at home about the Switzerland trip – knew it was no use. But Isobel said it was essential for Irene to go. They were best friends. After they became world-championship skaters they were going to join ice shows in America, saying they were a sister-team. They had it all worked out. She had to admire them. She was planning to give Irene her laundry money anyway, but it seemed small enough. Still, every little helps as the old lady said when she piddled in the sea.

She worked part-time, packing sheets and towels into large hampers for a few well-needed quid a week. Mrs Dawes sat for Warren, or Edward did.

She was excited about Irene going to Switzerland. She'd seen a picture of Mrozek's chalet in Paris Match, Edward had brought it as it featured European musicians. (Mrozek and Irene up on the ski slopes ?) She had a little vision of herself there, lying out on a balcony, dark glasses, the lot. *Just move that lot of sheets, Mrs,* a voice cried out while she was away, dreaming, sipping her Cinzano Bianco. The only bloody Alps she would see – that pile of sheets.

Yesterday Carole had learned a bit of 'Three Blind Mice' and that's what counted, not bloody Switzerland. Edward knew that. She and Edward.

'TED AND BILL WAS HERE. BALLOCKS.' Scrawled on their wall. People thought they'd gone. They put out a sign saying '*We are still here.*'

Irene thought it up. But it didn't stop a stone coming through Edward's window. He put in hardboard to stop the wind howling through.

(*And the swaying movements of the conductor's body, the arrogant point of a finger, the left hand – oh that left hand – held over the heart, to bring out the sweetness of the strings . . .*)

The supermarket was just about to close. She whizzed round. The cashier was chatting and the manager on the telephone in the back, so she stuffed two cans of soup and an instant coffee in her bag, then wheeled the rest round to the check-out. At the desk she slipped a bar of chocolate into her raincoat pocket.

What did it matter if she was arrested for shop-lifting – she wouldn't ever meet Mrozek, so what the hell . . .

(*And the swaying movements of the conductor's body . . .*)

Passed the Yogi's old ashram. Squatters were there now. God knows where he had gone. She missed him. Star of the Orient, the housewives' friend.

The squatters looked great. Edward had been right, as always. They should have had the guts to do it when he said. But they made her feel old. The girls, in Indian gear, with scarves wrapped round their heads, sat on the step. Kids swarmed. The men were bearded, beautiful. They seemed beautiful to her, all of them. Like gypsies. Terry wouldn't see the charm.

Edward had tried to interview them, but they told him to fuck off. She was glad. She was amazed to find she'd been a bit uneasy at the thought of him seeing those women there. Kind of stupid, jealousy about Edward. It was just she didn't know how she was going to manage without him.

She would have liked to be in charge of that crane up there, with its big ball, smashing into walls. Their walls, too, the squatters, with their slogans ... LOVE ... PINOCHET OUT TROOPS WITHDRAW, etc. What did it all matter? Knock it down, WHAM! POW! Like in the comics. Down with it all – the Festival Hall and the Law Courts and the bleeding Houses of Parliament and the posh restaurants and the whole bloody lot – who needed it?

And then what? Sweet nothing.

It would be worth it so see their faces – they'd say who did it, was it the IRA or the CIA or the UDA? And she'd say no, it was ME.

27

'Say ah, Carole, and then ooh.' Edward was firm.

'N-no ...' She squirmed in her chair.

'Say ah, Carole, for me. For Edward. I'll give you a sweetie, look ...

'Ah, ah.'

'No, longer. Aaaah. Then oooh.'

'Aah. Ooh.'

'Good girl. Here. Now, let's try bee. Here's your sweet.'

'Bee.'

'Great. Really good. For another sweet, yellow.'

'Bee. Buzz buzz.'

'Good, that's my girl, you've got it. Now, show me the card for the boy.'

'*Boy.*'

'Right. What's this, Carole? Think now . . . don't laugh just because mummy has come in.'

'Bell.'

'And this . . . ?'

'Apple.'

'Right. Rest a minute. God help her teeth,' said Edward. 'It's working though, isn't it?'

'Seems to be,' she said, grinning all over her face. Carole looked from one to the other, smiling.

'Back to work, Carole. What's this?'

'Pedro.'

'That's fantastic. She needs an extra sweet for that, doesn't she?'

She nodded, unable to speak.

'Dog,' said Carole, proudly. 'Dog dog dog . . .'

'Are you pleased,' he said, 'at her progress?'

'Pleased? I'm astounded.'

'Want a sweet?'

'Please . . .'

'Can't have one.'

'Don't be stupid, Edward.'

He could be a real tease. Carole watched, cheeks bulging.

'I'm the teacher,' he said, 'and I say "no".'

Just when you really liked him he played you up, he did it on purpose, to avoid emotion. She grabbed the bag.

'I took a green. Nobody seems to like them.'

'You try with her now.' Getting his own back.

'I can't – I wouldn't know where to start.'

'You'll have to when we all split up. Take a card and ask her to tell you the word on another.'

She picked up a picture of a telephone. Carole picked out a T.

She did word after word, picture after picture.

'You must praise her more,' he said. 'She needs it.'

It was a bit against her nature, but she managed.

One card Carole would not name. A baby.
'She won't do this one.'
'It could be jealousy of Warren . . . do you think?'
'But she *loves* Warren.'
'You can't tell.'
'Of course I can bloody tell. I've had three you know. It's Irene who is jealous. Carole gets all your attention, and Warren mine – *and* Warren being Terry's favourite . . . With families, it's hard to tell who is the scapegoat.'
'Men don't see things that clearly.'
'Family life is a bleedin' war, and don't you forget it.'
'What does that make me, a war correspondent?'
'Well, you'll soon be off to god knows where.'
'I'd rather not – you know that.'
He was scribbling something on one of Carole's cards. Scratched out the word giraffe, and wrote 'I love you.' He fished in his pocket and finally pulled out a snap of himself and put it over the giraffe, sticking it with a bit of Copydex. He handed it to her.
'I thought *I* was supposed to fit the word and the picture card,' she said.
'Just trying to help. Is it right?'
'I'm too dumb to know,' she said.

28

Terry came in with his overcoat all frosted – looked done in. She was baking bread, had started to do it as a sort of guilt reaction to her fantasies of betrayal. As if doing simple honest things like baking good bread (although they preferred Sunblest) would be some kind of atonement.
'Not that hard tack again,' said Terry.
She scrubbed the kitchen table, which Edward had pointed out to her, was extremely fine pine. So, she scrubbed it now.
(*Oh that left hand, that delicate left hand, held over the heart to . . .*)
'Make us a cup of tea, love.'

(Oh that sway of the body)

'Er . . . just see you label those sheets and towels properly, Mrs er . . .'

'Piss off.'

SHED AGRO on the laundry wall. SHIT TO RODNEY. Even them out of date. Old scrawls. Nearly home, shopping dragging her arms down. Like a gorilla. Hope they couldn't smell the laundry on her. Fuck them if they did. Everybody had to wash.

Even *him*.

29 Edward

Mother stayed at Ebury Street for a while, attending the hospital for treatments which left her lethargic and nauseous. She managed to trail around Fortnum's and Harrods when she wasn't laid out on my hide couch.

I managed somehow to fit her in with my family – she was used to my assignments. I took her out to lunch in the little restaurants that sprang up like flowers each spring. It seemed ironic that what we spent on these occasions would have supported the Wandsworth lot for a week. I had to stomach that fact, along with the lunch. Who could say which was more important, her sick palate; or the five I had begun to feel responsible for? It was a moral judgement my digestion took over – I had the beginnings of an ulcer.

The Major wasn't in evidence. She said vaguely he was a great help in the country – dogs and things. The echo of filial affection I showed her delighted her much more than the real thing would have done. She had always had a weakness for con men.

I knew she was dying. I knew she knew it too. She was too polite to mention it, so we filled in time together. The opera, concerts (once we heard Mrozek), the ballet, a couple of art shows. At all these places, bars, foyers, galleries, she glittered. I watched her try her ploys on unsuspecting males who swanned up to say hello.

Would she be in Scotland that summer? France? She kept up the illusion. I saw it give her the will to totter on. I recalled those harsh days of adolescence when I judged her with my teenaged puritanism. I despised my callow younger self at that moment.

One day, rushing back, I found her on the couch, smothered in flowers. A decorative corpse. There were no cards with the bouquets. With her usual logic, she had ordered them herself.

For days after that parcels and packages arrived. She had gone out on a massive spending spree. I returned them reluctantly.

Mrs Etherton said she had been rushing in and out like a mad thing. She had assumed there was to be a big party – all those flowers . . .

I asked the doctor when death had happened. I'd been playing Ludo with Irene and Carole at the kitchen table. I won.

I arranged cremation, for she had never expressed any desire to be buried. I searched in vain for any sort of message or note, just as I used to wait in vain for letters from her at school, knowing she would be too busy to write. I only hoped she was at some vast cocktail party in the sky.

My drawers, which she had taken over, were lined with perfumed paper – it would take me years to get rid of the pong. It would haunt me. Many invitations were stuck around my mantelpiece looking-glass. Her familiar leather writing case was open on my desk and a half-started letter read:

'Dear Rupert (the Major?), please see that Mr Dawson who cuts the hedges, is paid. I will reimburse you when I see you . . . I need to . . .' It finished there.

The Major came to the service. So did my father, the middle husband. The other two didn't turn up, though I put an obituary in *The Times*. Nor did any of her friends show – she wouldn't have expected them to.

My father, older and heavier, told me he had retired. He had been a local councillor for a couple of years, but now Bella was suffering from arthritis, and he was needed around the house.

When I caught sight of him he was studying the list of cremations for the day. Just seeing who she is going up with, she was always so fussy about guest lists, he said, ironically. On reflection, it was a remark she would have liked. It showed he had improved. She once told me she could get a divorce from him on the grounds of humourlessness, had there been such a category.

We sat, the Major, my father, myself, all in separate pews. The sun shone down rather theatrically.

The chapel of rest was discreet, inoffensive, in good taste. Flowers were laid outside in rows; there were a few personal ones on the actual pine coffin, which waited there.

The Major appeared to be crying; on the other hand he could have been a sufferer from hay-fever. My father looked at the ceiling, and then at his nails. A few bars of electronic hymn music flowed out after the little speech, and, like a 'thirties cinema organ, the coffin slid delicately out of sight, backing out through velvet curtains. I felt she would have appreciated that – she who had attended so many premieres, charity film shows and benefits. Now she was the star turn. A pity it was so ill-attended. Still, she had had the last devious word, like a naughty hostess she had put together the Major, father and myself. Let them get on with it, she used to say – and we would have to.

I looked across at dad. Alone at last, I thought. She, him and me. Except that, as in earlier days, there was still a stranger there, hovering. She would be a Noel Coward kind of spirit, I thought, wondered if dad was thinking the same.

Bella was in the car, he told me. The next lot were waiting to move in. Want to say hello ? he asked. I couldn't really refuse. She felt it wasn't right to come in, he said. Your mother never liked her.

I thought she'd been very wise. The ghost of my mama would have flitted around her, laughing at that hat. I put my hand in the car, and Bella shook it. We mouthed promises to meet. I said I would visit Mortlake – 'a warm welcome awaits' he said. My mother always accused him of talking like a cheap greeting card. 'Here's our little bundle of joy, then . . .' she told me he said on my arrival at the London Clinic.

He was thrilled by the amount of flowers outside. More than anyone else got. She was, he said, that kind of woman. They were taking up all the other spaces, had I noticed ? Some of them were from very important people – had I noticed ? I said I had. 'Douglas Fairbanks', 'André Malraux', 'Willy Brandt.' I had been very inventive.

All those famous men – he shook his head sadly. Like her dinner parties. (I wondered if it was an offence, writing wreath cards that were lies.) I was too quiet for her, he finally said, hand on the car door

Nonsense, she was very fond of you. (Had *those two* been in charge of my life ?)

Gave my address, scrawled on my bank statement. Good-bye, *good-bye . . .*

The Major needed succour too. Shared my cab. He settled on the tip-up seat opposite and said he didn't wish to be undignified, but there was something he felt obliged to – It sounded like a financial request to me.

As I expected. Solomon, Sheba and their insatiable appetites were mentioned, also the gardener. I felt for my cheque book. He apologized (old chap) for bringing it up.

What better time to settle things, I said. We travelled through Pimlico and the King's Road, jammed as usual with life. It was as exuberant as her passing had been dull. She should have been buried here, or Sloane Square.

I made out a cheque for twenty pounds, noticing the Major's down-at-heel shoes. The old cuss looked distinctly sad I thought. Perhaps there had been something between them after all.

He asked me suddenly if she owned the house in Orford. I realized he might be expecting a legacy of some kind.

On an impulse I offered him her old car – said she had mentioned he would like it. I lied.

(Afterwards I could have kicked myself. If anyone needed a car it was *my* family in Wandsworth, but they would never have afforded the upkeep.) I said I would be down to sort out mother's things, and we would go into all that then. Already I could hear sardonic tones in my ear: '*Beware the first instinct, it is always a generous one.*' *Talleyrand.*

What about Solomon and Sheba, I queried, having just shelled out twenty pounds for their upkeep.

The housekeeper said it was alright to leave them in your flat, he sighed. Popped them in on the way to the funeral. Did I know they cost half-fare, just like children ? *First class*, too, he insisted. I was beginning to admire the man.

Somewhere along King's Road he grabbed the door handle and after tapping the glass to get the driver to stop, he leapt out. I have a lunch date at Don Luigi's, he shouted at me, slamming the door. He didn't wave.

Back in the flat Solomon and Sheba huddled together, whining.

30

She was surprised to find Edward in the kitchen, sitting there with a huge bottle of that white Italian wine he liked so much. He was a regular addict, he didn't wait for a meal, just drank it, like water from the tap. He seemed depressed.

'You been up to London?' she said.

'A service for a friend,' He swigged straight from the bottle.

'We do have glasses.'

'Get yourself one, and join me?'

'Here,' she said, handing him two tumblers. 'Not too much, I don't like getting tiddly in the afternoon.'

He didn't speak, just handed her a brimming glass.

'How's the article coming along, then?' she asked. 'I told my friend about it and she said no one took that long to turn out an article.'

'Ah, well, it is more a series,' he said. He did look drunk, all red around the eyes. 'You know,' he suddenly remarked, swinging around to face her, 'you know, if you peered into the minds of your feverish feminine sisters while your precious Mrozek was conducting, do you know what it would be like?'

She didn't know what he was on about. He looked so vicious.

'A festering swamp.' He drank another glass down.

She laughed. Humour him. Always the best thing to do with drunks.

'Oh, yes?' she said, sipping delicately.

'A swamp of unfulfilled desires, all bubbling to the music of poor old Gustave, or Ludwig.'

'I know, but why does it bother you?' The wine had gone to her head, her cheeks were on fire.

'I hate to see you mooning about.'

'I'm not mooning about. I'm getting on with my life. Such as it is.'

'You're a sensible woman. Do something, don't be like all those dreary stockbrokers' wives who go to the concerts and the opera and ooze about Giulini. They throw pots in their pottery classes and do good works.'

'I'm not like them. That's why I haven't gone to art classes in the evening.'

'Then paint, dammit. You say you want to.'

'You're drunk, Edward Rayburn.'

'Not. Slightly sozzled, I'll admit to. Not drunk. Forget the bloody music. Would you like to go to the opera – have you ever been to the opera?'

She shook her head. He went rambling on; something about her Mrozek obsession was making him angry. She filled up her own glass, more to protect him than anything else. Just to stop him having more.

'Were you joking about the opera?'

'No,' he said. He'd get tickets. Then she could see all the matrons, sitting there creaming their pants like Bowie fans, for *Mrozek*.

'Dirty-minded sod,' she remarked mildly.

'They have their balding slaves sitting next to them, they have flogged out pounds for the seats. *Mrozek!* they cry, into their pillows. Then, no, I have a headache, when poor Cyril wants to exert his marital post-opera rights . . .'

'Silly bugger,' she said.

'Don't you become like that . . .' He grabbed her by the wrist. Hard. She pulled away.

'Fat chance.'

'You know what I mean, don't live in your head.'

'Where else is there to live. Here?'

He did a strange thing: he pressed the glass in his hand, until it broke and the blood streamed down his fingers.

She ran it under the cold tap. Got the splinters of glass out for him. Bandaged it up. He looked pale and sick.

'What did you want to do that for, silly boy . . .'

Men. They were all the same.

31 Edward

I went to Ebury Street, collected mail from Mrs E. My editor wanted me to go to Germany next month.

Do I have any relationships, except with *them* (Her.) Christ – I have to get used to losing her.

Mrs E. grumbled about Solomon and Sheba. They were left too much, they barked. The other tenants were complaining.

I told her I exercised them twice a day, which was untrue. It was an improbable and impossible situation. I went back and forth to Wandsworth like a yo-yo. No one wanted me there, particularly. The dogs wanted me here.

I told Mrs E. a couple from Surbiton were coming to take Solomon and Sheba. Sheba jumped up and started masturbating my leg at the thought of the couple from Surbiton, while Solomon, who had been more attached to my mother, stayed put, sulking.

Mrs E. had been marvellous, I thought. The place didn't smell bad at all, and they didn't seem too plump. She must be subsidizing their exercise. Then she told me. Miss Anya had been in, and taken them out daily. She and my old girl friend got along. Yapping about animal vivisection and Beauty without Cruelty.

I bent to pat Sheba, who was sniffing my shoe, smelling Pedro, no doubt. Talk of the devil – Anya rushed in, doing her breathless thing. She flung her arms around my neck.

Anya looked hurt when I recoiled slightly. Tactful Mrs E. withdrew, tossing mental bridal bouquets into the room.

'Mrs E. rang me – I've been taking them in the Park every day,' Anya pouted. 'The taxi is waiting. Are you coming with us?'

'As far as I am concerned,' I said, 'they can jump in the lake.'

'But they do. They love it.'

They shook water over us as they emerged, making Anya giggle. I had forgotten what it was like to walk with the blonde beanpole. People smiled and stared – she had been on so many commercials. Have you ever seen an ad. walking?

I was beginning to feel as ersatz as mock cream.

I could remember a time when I enjoyed this instant notoriety. How I had changed. I wondered if it was an improvement. Probably not.

I recalled our love scenes. Scenes I called them, deliberately. Mock-ups for a camera rehearsal. She couldn't help it. She started young, known as the Tigress, flaunting her mane and her teeth. I wondered how she managed now she was vegetarian. What kind of homely vegetable would I be? A turnip, I thought. I wasn't exotic enough to be an aubergine, or even a carrot.

'What are you thinking?'

'I was thinking *I am a turnip.*'

'Who is she?'

'Who is *who*?'

'Your new dolly.'

'Impossible girl,' I said. 'I have no dolly. I'm going through the male menopause.'

'But you're only thirty.' Her face darkened.

'What are you doing, beside walking my dogs?'

She had done a session in Paris. What was I doing apart from amusing my new dolly?

'I have gone free-lance in spite of VAT,' I said. To put her off, really. She was bored by tax. She asked if I was still on the diet connected with my birth sign she'd worked out for me.

'Of course I am.'

'Then why are you so pale and spotty?'

I thought of the corned beef and cabbage, the chocolate cup cakes, the peanut butter sandwiches, the chips and beans and bacon.

'I'm well-trained by you, Anya . . I could never go back to eating all that muck.'

She kissed me. A young chap with an Afghan could have castrated me, so envious was he.

'I must get back,' she said. 'It's my Dance Centre morning.'

'Still improving yourself? You don't need it . . .'

She pretended always not to notice the men staring.

'All those beastly lustful men. Staring. Ugh.' She smiled with satisfaction.

'Taxi! Solomon – Sheba . . .'

They curled up, exhausted, on the back seat.

'You won't have to do this again,' I said. 'A couple from Surbiton...'

'I think you are going to do them in. I wish dogs could talk.'

I was glad they could not.

'You know, you've been seen around with the most frightful old slag.'

I slapped her across her beautiful cheek.

The taxi-driver drew up and ordered me out; he punched me in the jaw. I didn't bother to defend myself, I was too busy trying to get hold of Solomon and Sheba. As the taxi drove off I stepped on Solomon, who promptly bit me in the ankle. I kicked him in the rear end. A passing old lady hit me with her unbrella, threatening to call the police. I asked the small crowd who had gathered if they would like to adopt two dachshunds. I hailed a taxi, only to be told he didn't want dogs in his cab.

Solomon, Sheba and I walked back to Ebury Street. Mrs E. hardly spoke, showed no sympathy. Anya had been, and gone.

'You've lost a lovely girl, there, Mr Rayburn. She even tried to make the little dogs into vegetarians, but they didn't take to it. Don't you leave them here. I won't have them if Miss Anya isn't coming in.'

I pleaded, just until tomorrow, but it was no use. Said she would report me to the management, who didn't officially like pets. Or the RSPCA. I protested that I had been bitten, punched and hit over the head with an umbrella. Surely I deserved a bit of her concern. She said it was all right for me, I was human.

I bathed my chin in the bathroom and stuck a plaster on Solomon's bite. Changed into my St Laurent jeans and jacket – I had no others. The ones I had been wearing were covered in blood and dog saliva.

I almost believed in the reality of the couple from Surbiton myself as I attempted to leave nonchalantly, with Solomon and Sheba trotting smartly on separate leads.

I marched off with my doggy twins. I didn't know where to go. I could hardly appear with them in Wandsworth – it would be difficult to explain my new clobber in a house where nothing new entered from week to week.

My mother had a special veterinary surgeon somewhere near Sloane Square. His receptionist was cool, but said he might fit us in at twelve. He was doing a tricky tooth operation on an alsatian at the moment.

I tried to get into various coffee bars, but no one would have them. The pubs were not open. We sat, watching the world go by.

'Look here,' I said, before he had time to shake hands, 'I want to get rid of them. They were so attached to my mama . . . they will never tolerate anyone else.'

'They seem quite fond of you,' he remarked. He felt their squirming bellies. 'They are in the pink you know, very fine, expensive dogs.'

'I have to fly off – today . . . I can't have them. I have to interview the President.'

'Which one?'

'Does it matter?' I wasn't even capable of getting rid of the little horrors.

On the train back to Wandsworth I considered the pros and cons of the situation.

One: I had not been as brutal as I might have been. Therefore my conscience was clearer. Two: I felt a stupid ass. I had attempted to palm them off on him, and then I tried to sell them, at which suggestion he was very insulted. Three: I ended up paying twenty-five quid a week at an exclusive boarding kennels, where they will live the life of Riley. He probably gets a percentage.

Do I realize that she gets less than that for a week's housekeeping?

I do.

Do I find myself ridiculous?

I do . . .

32

She got out the little tubes of oil paints and the piece of hardboard, she primed the hardboard and then she sat there. She splashed a load of white base, mixed in the cake tin, over the so-called canvas and then she did a large pink blob.

Warren, who was being bribed to sit at the table, shrieked to be let down.

She pushed another bar of milk chocolate across at him. He got his book out, and pretended to read, chocolate fingermarks all over the outside. She couldn't really see his face, but it was no good having a row with him, he was quiet now.

She got in the outline, forming his shape. Doing a splash of blue for his dungarees, and a dot for each blue eye. It was beginning to shape up. Edward was right. You should do something yourself. She fiddled around with the angle of the head, just a wash of pink, a kind of childishness, but not too simple.

It was great, messing about with colours this way. Edward had said, just go off, get some oil paints and do it. Take the rent money. Don't try and go to evening classes – just *do it*. Lots of artists were self-taught.

An hour passed. She was totally involved. She forgot to do the potatoes. Warren was dozing, head on the table. She had scrubbed out the first picture, and covered the hardboard with white background again. Now she was well away – a sleeping child.

The door rattled. She put her brush down carefully and went. Irene stood there. And Carole. They looked at her accusingly.

'What happened?' said Irene.

'I didn't notice the time. Anyway, you are big girls now. You can get home yourselves.'

'*She* was upset.' Irene looked across at Carole. 'She likes you to come.'

'I know she does. She'll get used to it. She'll come on the bus when she goes to the special school.'

'Is this what you've been doing?' Irene looked at it critically.

'It's just rough.' She started to pack up.

'Is it meant to be *Warren*?' Irene's voice went up in incredulous disbelief.

'More just an impression of a child sleeping.'

'Miss Arundel is a good painter.'

'Is she?'

'She went to the Harrow School of Art.'

'Did she?'

It was no use. She bunged it all into the back of the cupboard.

Warren was very red in the face. He puked up a chocolate mess on to the table.

'*Someone's* been giving Warren loads of chocolate,' Irene said, going for a bowl and a cloth.

33 Edward

Found her in the kitchen, reading, fag in hand, a can of beer on the table beside her. She ignored me; went on reading.

'Why are the girls crying? Carole seems upset.'

'What's it to do with you? You are out all the time. She isn't your responsibility.'

I didn't have to take that shit – I wasn't the husband, the father. But I just said, what was wrong?

It was Pedro, and the cat. Apparently they couldn't go to the high-rise block. She'd known for ages, but she had just revealed it to the girls.

'They aren't that fond of the cat – it's never in,' I said. Neither are you, her eyes implied.

'Can't I help?' I said, foolishly, it turned out.

She looked at me with her cool gaze.

'Perhaps you can,' she said.

I looked at her objectively. An old slag, Anya said. She did look weary, her period probably. I realized with a pang that I knew her better, more intimately, than those I had slept with, for they had always kept some exclusive part of themselves for themselves. Kept their defences in trim. She had none. Her hair needed washing. Old slag? Anya didn't know the half of it.

'Let me help you,' I said. 'I can, you know . . .'

She looked up, dull eyes, heavy lidded. Without her knowing it, during our brief conversation she had lit up from within – she couldn't remain down for longer than five minutes.

'Where in hell's name have you been? And where did you get that clobber?'

That was more like it. Laughing, she looked at the label.

'Come into money? You look great.'

She meant it, I could see her double-take, perhaps if she knew someone like me, she might not be too removed from . . .

'Let's go out somewhere, I promised to take you to the opera.'

'Who, me?'

'Mrozek is conducting *Figaro*. I'll get tickets.'

'But–'

'No buts. I'll hire a proper babysitter. And, don't worry about Pedro and the cat. I'll fix that too.'

I must be mad.

'Edward –'

'What?'

'I don't know what I would do without you. And, Edward, you won't mind if I go in my ordinary skirt?'

'Look,' I said, pulling out some notes from my pocket, 'take a taxi – go to Putney, and buy yourself something, a long dress.'

I couldn't . . .'

'Go on. I'll get their tea . . .'

Surprisingly, she went. I looked at myself in the kettle. Distorted Sir Lancelot.

34

She felt odd, riding in a taxi, Edward's fivers in her bag. Looked out at shop windows with a different eye. Actually it had crossed her mind to grab something for the kids, but Edward would be furious if she did. He would know if she didn't spend it all. It was worrying her, too, what Terry would say. After all, buying her clothes. What would he think? But this was the real test – was it worth risking? It was worth risking for Mrozek.

The taxi-man winked as she tipped him fifty pence. Was it too much? It was probably written all over her face that she never took taxis. She had to try on with lots of other women; for a moment she felt ashamed, but no one looked at her. They were all so *thin*. She chose something that looked Indian, a long red and cream flowered dress. She did look nice in it. She had enough for a bit of perfume. And a taxi home.

Edward was washing Warren at the sink. She put the dress on, paraded in front of them all. Irene said she looked beautiful. Even Terry, when he came in, wasn't put out. She said she'd spent the rent money. Edward was in his room, of course, so Terry didn't connect him with it.

She asked what Terry was doing Friday. Darts match, he said. A friend wanted her to go out. Why don't you then? he said. So that was settled.

Friday, this old lady with a limp and bi-focals turned up. She had been a nanny. Took a look at the place and nearly fainted. Irene made her a cup of tea. She heard the ex-Nanny asking Edward details of the bathroom, kitchen and so on. Edward was doing his best to charm her.

The ex-nanny said she was used to a car home, and where was the telephone? Edward promised her a mini-cab.

She kissed the girls. Edward was pacing up and down, Warren was bedded. She hated leaving them with that dragon.

She saw Carole's face fall as she started towards the door. Edward pulled her out of the front passage. Slam.

'You'll have to forget them all for one night,' he said.

Miserable as sin, she was, already.

35 Edward

She clutched my hand as the lights dimmed and the dark figure of Mrozek emerged in the pit. Then she floated away from me as surely as she did when she was in one of her dark, pessimistic moods, of which I had suffered many.

I realized, for the first time, seeing her this way, in my sort of surroundings, that my interest – which I had supposed was social, or political, or humane, was total. It included love, sex – all. It had taken a new dress, a touch of perfume, Mozart ... and that was it. I thought the subdued and subordinate the attraction of the relationship – the physicality of her I knew was there since the kitchen strip. But now, spiritually, if I could think of it that way, she seemed mine. I had never thought to desire her in this particular way. Our psyches were clicked together, like lock and key. We were one – and I had never had her.

Her passion for Mrozek created sexual jealousy of a kind I'd never had before. I watched her watch him. It was painful sitting next to her. The duet between the Count and Susannah had never seemed to me so tragically balanced on the knife-edge between desire and duplicity.

She watched herself coming down the grand staircase in the interval, reflected, and asked me if she looked as if she belonged.

I said I quite understood.

I didn't want the evening to end.

It was like the first time for me through her innocent eyes. She generated excitement, through every pore.

In the taxi as we went back to reality via Waterloo Bridge she chattered about Mrozek incessantly. Covent Garden, and Mozart, until I stopped her mouth with a sudden kiss. It was like my first girl – a closed mouth kiss, tender and gentle. Then we drew up at 13, Huntsmore Road.

36

They made their way into the throng of people.

The noise, the scent of the crowd intoxicated her much more than the vodka and tonic Edward bought at the bar. (She had asked him if they could buy some chocolate at the kiosk near the cloakroom, but he said it would melt, and couldn't she forget them for a while; nevertheless she managed to get some while he was in the cloakroom, she stuffed them in her bag so he wouldn't know.) She was glad to see the last of her tweed coat – it reeked of chips.

In her new dress she seemed like everyone else.

The barman had said to Edward, 'the usual, sir?' Meaning, she supposed, that he had been here often, with other women. Edward took care to find out if she did in fact want vodka. She hoped he wasn't bored coming with her. She didn't have any small talk. He seemed satisfied.

It was so funny, sad and erotic, all at the same time. She didn't see how the singers could contain all this – and Mrozek, holding it all together. The core of the magic. She watched his hands, urging, softening. The voices rose, fell, blended at his command. Her cheeks reddened because Edward was looking at her. Or maybe he wanted to leave – perhaps it was a bad performance and she did not know. Oh, no – she knew it wasn't. It was brilliant. She glanced at Edward and he looked away.

She thought she would never retain a hold on all this, but later, in the taxi, she found she could hum the tune the Countess, poor sad thing, sang about love at the beginning of the second act. Edward suddenly gave her a brotherly kiss on the mouth. He certainly had been kind, he had probably seen this opera many times, and it was good of him to seem interested. She asked him about other times. He said this was the best.

Maybe it was someone else's first time too. She hoped it had been. Some nice young girl.

She wondered what Mrozek did afterwards.

They opened the door. The nanny had gone off in her mini-cab, Terry was back. A bit pissed, he was, but he made them a pot of tea. She told him about it all. He seemed quite interested and he thanked Edward for taking her. Then he got angry and he took her by the shoulders and shook her. She'd told him she was going with a friend. Edward *is* a friend, she cried.

Terry said he would give him until the end of the week to get his things out.

37 Edward

The girls in the outer office of the veterinary surgeon's office giggled.

'He's here again. He's got two more.'

'What have you got in the basket?'

'Actually, it is a very old cat. Mangy, disreputable; unable to be re-housed by the Council.'

'You'll be bringing in your old mother next,' she said. 'Two dachshunds the other day, for the chop, now these. Who is this lovely fellow?'

Pedro held up his paw. She shook it.

'He's for the chop too,' I said. No good beating around the bush. 'It's better than letting them off on the motorway, like some. He's had a good life.'

'Virtuous, aren't we . . .' she said.

'They aren't mine. I'm doing it for a friend.'

'They all say that, don't they, Maeve?'

Pedro lifted his leg against the desk.

'Ooh, naughty,' said Maeve. 'I'd have him, but I'm in a bed-sitter.'

'They all say that, too. Why don't you take pity on me?'

'I'd have you done in like a shot,' said Maeve.

It was only after I had watched Pedro's last tremors I realized the question of a posh boarding kennel for him had not come up. The vet said the dog was past it. Anyway, it was someone else's, wasn't it? I asked how those two sycophants, Solomon and Sheba, were getting on. Thriving, I was told.

He said he could do the cat later, so I wrote out a cheque. He handed me Pedro's collar. I shook my head.

'Tell me again,' said Irene, that night. Carole sat up in bed too.

'Well, we finally got off the train and saw all those lovely fields stretching out . . .'

'No sheep, because Pedro chases sheep.'

'There were a few. Pedro was very good. The farmer said he might train him as a sheep dog, in fact. He'd just lost his.'

'Lost his? You mean it died?'

'Oh no. It refused to work, so it had to – ' God, I was getting confused.

'I hope he is better with Pedro. That old farmer.' Irene was looking at me with scorn. I wondered if I had altered any details since the last telling.

'Can you remember what he said to me then?'

'No visits,' said Irene, straightening her quilt. 'Right, Carole?'

'That was a condition – otherwise he wouldn't settle.'

Carole was mouthing 'Puss.'

'Oh, and the cat would be very useful. Lots of mice in the barn.'

I looked at them both.

'I hope they don't work them too hard,' said Irene, snuggling down. 'Pedro is . . . was very lazy, you know.'

'They'll train him,' I said, tucking her in. I kissed Carole.

'It's almost too good to be true, isn't it?'

The ironic shrill voice of Irene followed me down the stairs.

In the kitchen she pushed a can of light ale at me.

'For services rendered,' she said. 'I wish you wouldn't tell them stories about it. Irene's old enough to know about death.'

'I don't think Irene believes me anyway. She is playing along.'

'I don't know, you're quite the romancer. Very believable.'

I grabbed her by the wrist. Harder than I intended.

'They need their fantasies just as much as you do – '

She reddened.

'Well, thanks again.' Cool, formal.

'I'm good for some things, at any rate.'

'You are good for lots of things. Don't underestimate yourself all the time.'

She ruffled my hair. My scalp burned all day. It was the first affectionate gesture I had inspired from her.

38

She was standing outside Mrozek's house, she didn't know why, her shopping bag loaded with dog and cat food – she picked them up automatically, as if Pedro and Puss still existed.

It was one of those grey days when you felt the world might end out of sheer indifference. The rain slanting down. Why was she here? She didn't know for certain that he was even in this country. He went through countries like a knife through butter – here, there, god knows where. When Edward left she wouldn't even get the information. *The Marriage of Figaro* had finished. She was still here.

She'd left Warren with Edward. That too would change. The kids would miss him.

The black front door seemed firmly shut, as if no one lived there. The bay tree in the wooden tub shivered in the wind.

It went round and round, what Edward had said, that you mustn't live in your head. It was a sin. But where else was there, when reality was so dull?

Terry would be back. She would have liked to curl up on the step, to have gone to sleep.

For ever and ever, amen. Near.

She started off, but the cans of cat and dog meat weighed her down. She got one out of her bag, meaning to leave it somewhere – then, on a sudden whim she threw it. It landed down in the area, where the dustbin was, where her letter had been.

A second one she threw at an upper window. Marie-Helène's bedroom, she hoped. It broke the pane with a sharp crack, the glass shattered down over the bay tree.

Silence. It was an exclusive, deserted area.

She looked around. Not a sign. Not even a car going past. She threw another, just for the hell of it. It bounced off a window sill, on to the pavement and rolled into the gutter. Her bag was much lighter now. She moved off.

A police car drew up beside her. The young policeman asked her if she had noticed anything unusual. They had received a telephone call from one of the embassies. A bomb scare. Had she seen anything strange? No, she said. Nothing. They asked to look in her bag, she opened the shopping up. He touched his cap and drove off, giving her a nice smile.

The funny thing was, she felt as if she'd actually fucked Mrozek. Her pants were wet with excitement.

39 Edward

Well, I have done it. Betrayed myself and her. The desecration I always allow myself when in love. It wasn't the first time, and I don't suppose it will be the last . . .

Oh, yes. What to do now? Complete the rape by completing the article? Why not? Her strength is still my problem, she is likely to forgive me, to try and understand me. To give: the only thing she knows how to do. I wouldn't be able to stand that.

How comfortable it will be, back in my negative land where I don't have to pretend that life is possible. The bloody old eternal feminine nearly had me that time, Goethe-baby.

Well, back to cynicism.

And yet, when I hear a touch of the old Mahler schmalz, a blast on those Wagner tubas, I will think of her. When I see a face pressed to the window in one of those tower blocks that are mushrooming up all over Europe, I shall be unable to put her out of my mind.

I never used her name, she never seemed to have one.

She was very ordinary, a sort of Woolworth madonna. There must be millions like her.

40

Edward came into her bedroom. He had been drinking. He said to move out Warren's cot because he wanted to fuck her. She said don't be silly, Terry would be back, he was only down at the pub. But he said Terry was involved in a darts match, and wouldn't be back just yet. And wasn't Saturday night the working-class night for a fuck?

She was rather scared then, and said they should go down for a coffee, and he followed her down. Pale he was, and very grim, not a happy drunk, like some. She put on her old blue dressing gown, and tucked Warren in.

Edward was in his room, lying on the camp bed when she took it in. He threw the coffee across the room against the wall. The brown liquid went right down the poster of Mrozek, down his face, and she rushed to the kitchen for a cloth and began dabbing it. She got angry at what he had done, and punched him with her fists.

He grabbed her arm and pulled her down on him and forced her mouth on his, biting her lips inside. It was painful. Yet she, in spite of herself, got carried away by the intensity of his tongue and his body. It was as if he wanted to imprint himself on her for ever. She was not used to being on top of a man and he was so wiry and insistent, not like Terry.

Fear was her main emotion, fear that he might do something violent if she refused, and also the fear that the girls would hear. Terry would kill her, kill them both if he came in.

Each time she tried to lessen the impetus he forced her further and finally twisted suddenly and was on top of her. He tore off her dressing gown and lifted her nightdress and entered her, but brutally. She couldn't scream, Carole was such a light sleeper. And he said that's all I ever wanted from you, *you cunt*. And he cried. She tried to be tender, and stop the force by holding him gently and saying there, there ... but that seemed to enrage him even more – and yet he didn't come. There was no hope of her responding; she felt so worried about him. Part of her body wanted to engage him in the fight, but she looked up and saw the dark eyes of Mrozek looking down on her. (*His hand held in suspension, the left one – oh, that left hand, which brought in the strings* ...)

Edward, in his climax, left her. Ejaculated on the bed. She held him, rocked him like a baby. So they remained until closing time. Then she whispered that Terry would be back, left him. She went upstairs. Warren and girls had not stirred.

In the kitchen she had a good wash, down there. When Terry got back she pretended to be asleep. He dropped his shoes on to the floor. One – two. She took no notice.

When she went down in the morning Edward had gone, cleared out, taking all his things.

She thought: it's all we have got, the world as it is, a great big muddle and us in the midst of it all. When she was a child on a train she cried because she saw all the houses, trees, roads passing – had wanted so much to be part of other people – felt she would die if she didn't find out how they lived, love them, and move on again, letting others know her, and so on, throughout the entire world. But you got beaten down by your own bit of territory, your own particular life.

Then you didn't get that expansive feeling any more, it died a little each day; when it came back it was with despair, and you let go, finally, realizing you couldn't do anything about it.

You couldn't get in touch with the whole world. It was only ever done in a masculine political way – exploitation. Not her way. She used to think why was she born feminine, white, in a country which had outlived its potential. She would never know what it would be to be in another world, another skin. Another time, another way.

But somehow you accepted it. As you did your own body. You had to accept it. The fact you hadn't done much you had to accept too – and the not reaching out, that you had to accept as well. And that some may reach out more and maybe they will be your children.

She lived here and now, in this time, this place. Nothing very much, but all she'd got.

Our life is bounded in a little ring and many generations are constantly succeeding each other like links in the endless chain of their existence. So said the young Goethe quoted by Edward. (He was always quoting Goethe.)

Her mouth still swollen, hurt. She puzzled over Edward, for how could the flesh of one man hurt another human being's flesh? Just that alone, no weapons? Yet men often used the body as a weapon. Perhaps they destroyed in war because of that. Once you had felt it slip out from between your legs, you couldn't use it that way. Women let men into their bodies, to embrace, enfold and receive them.

She would never know if Edward hated her, or why. She thought he understood her. Perhaps he hated understanding her.

She saw Mrozek was conducting on Friday night (Beethoven's Ninth). It seemed he had gone off Mahler.

Next week they would move into the flat. It would be different at least. A new life.

Carole said (clearly) 'colour television'. Terry was that pleased he said he would get one when they moved. Trade in the old set.

Warren went to the play group for the first time, for a whole morning session.

He banged on the drum. Went straight for it.

'Perhaps he is musical?' she said.

'Perhaps he is . . .' Miss White the infant teacher replied.

More about Penguins and Pelicans

For further information about books available from Penguins please write to Dept EP, Penguin Books Ltd, Harmondsworth, Middlesex UB7 0DA.

In the U.S.A.: For a complete list of books available from Penguins in the United States write to Dept CS, Penguin Books, 625 Madison Avenue, New York, New York 10022.

In Canada: For a complete list of books available from Penguins in Canada write to Penguin Books Canada Ltd, 2801 John Street, Markham, Ontario L3R 1B4.

In Australia: For a complete list of books available from Penguins in Australia write to the Marketing Department, Penguin Books Australia Ltd, P.O. Box 257, Ringwood, Victoria 3134.

A selection of women writers in Penguins

Fay Weldon

Down Among the Women

'Men are irrelevant. Women are happy or unhappy, fulfilled or unfulfilled and it has nothing to do with men.'

So says Fay Weldon in her striking, witty and sharply perceived novel. Her women are indeed battered by life but most of them are tough and resilient and manage to survive – willy-nilly – the disappointments, the love affairs and the broken marriages.

Alison Lurie

Only Children

Using the same stylish, tender and comic approach as in her bestselling *War Between the Tates*, Alison Lurie turns her attention to the goings-on one weekend on an idyllic upstate New York farmhouse, when the Hubbards and the Zimmerns – plus their children – come to stay with Anna. As Mary Ann and her friend Lolly play their games of make-believe something happens to the adults. It is as though there is a magic spell on the house which turns everybody in it into children – and only the children can see it.

Susan Hill

Gentleman and Ladies

Miss Faith Lavender would not have cried at her own funeral. And indeed no one attending the service shed a tear – neither her two sisters, nor the handful of neighbours, not the strange man in black boots holding stolen snowdrops. Faith Lavender's funeral and the arrival of a stranger upset the finely tuned balance of the little community. Undercurrents of fierce emotion, that until now have been suppressed, reach the surface while the tensions rise and the ladies of Haverstock find their actions motivated by mutual suspicion and fear.

Jean Rhys

Voyage in the Dark

A brief liaison with a kindly but unimaginative man leads Anna to abandon the theatre and drift into the demi-monde of 1914 London: red-plush dinners in private rooms 'up West'; ragtime, champagne and whisky back at the flat; these, and a discreet tinkle of sovereigns in the small hours pave the way to disaster . . .

Barbara Pym

Excellent Women

Mildred was quite capable of dealing with the stock situations of life. In fact her handling of births, marriages, deaths, jumble sales and garden fêtes ruined by the weather was masterly. It is the introduction of new and exotic neighbours that pulls her up short.
Barbara Pym is a rare and subtle writer. Unerring, acerbic, penetrating, she unravels with deceptive gentleness a world that is still part of the English social scene.

Elizabeth Bowen

The Death of the Heart

This book is perhaps Elizabeth Bowen's masterpiece. In it she deftly and delicately exposes the cruelty of cold and conventional people of fashion when sixteen-year-old Portia comes to live with her wealthy half-brother and his wife, Anna, in London during the 'thirties. Portia, tormented by the agonies of her first love-affair, is obsessed by the feeling that people are laughing at her: on discovering that Anna has been reading her diary she takes a sudden explosive step which pulls everyone up short.